Hiding Behind The Couch Series

by
Debbie McGowan

Beaten Track
www.beatentrackpublishing.com

Red Hot Christmas

First published 2014 by Beaten Track Publishing
Copyright © 2014–2023 Debbie McᶜGowan

Paperback ISBN: 978 1 78645 331 0
eBook ISBN: 978 1 909192 74 4

Original Cover Design: Natasha Snow
https://natashasnow.com

Beaten Track Publishing,
Burscough. Lancashire.
www.beatentrackpublishing.com

Contents

1. Ice Cold Sober 1

2. Against the Rocks 9

3. Bitters 17

4. Seeing Red 25

5. Rekindled Flame 33

6. Goodwill 41

7. Candy-Caned 53

8. Not Even a Peep 65

9. Deep Red Sea 75

10. Sleighride 91

11. Christmas Present 103

About the Author 118

By the Author 119

Beaten Track Publishing 122

1. Ice Cold Sober

I T WAS THE twenty-first of December, and the usual optimistic prediction for snow was showing in multiple definitions and sizes across the back-wall display of the electronics superstore. The zoom in and out of the map was vertiginous enough on a singular sixty-inch screen, never mind so many, the varying degrees of colour saturation and barely detectable delays putting some of them slightly out of sync from the rest.

Shaunna ignored the fullness of her bladder and shifted her gaze from the mesmeric screens, slowly rotating on the spot to survey the entirety of the enormous shop. Still no sign, and at a muscular six foot two, he wasn't exactly difficult to spot—if he was there to be spotted. She checked the time on her phone—discovering that a whole two minutes had passed since she last checked, making it 18:52—and chewed her lip, deep in the thoughts of all the possible reasons for the hold-up. It wasn't like him; it was usually she who kept him waiting.

"Are you OK there?"

The voice brought her back with a start. She turned and saw a *boy* in shop uniform standing by. He gave her a hopeful, nervous smile.

When did they get so young? "Yes, thanks. I'm just looking."

He nodded in relief and scooted off to loiter at the other end of the aisle of microwave ovens. Shaunna checked the time again: 18:53.

At what point should she give up waiting? She'd called his phone, twice, left voicemail and two text messages, all eliciting no response. The best explanation, certainly her favoured one, was that his phone was off or had no signal. The alternative involved his inability to stick to the speed limit and icy roads, and she didn't want to think about that. He was a risk-taker, adventure sports fanatic, lover of fast cars and life in the fast lane, but he could be sensible when he needed to be. The last few months had proved that beyond doubt.

"Are you interested in any model in particular?"

A different voice this time—female, though still young and equally as startling in her current contemplative state.

"Model?" Shaunna queried vaguely. She looked down and found she was holding open the door of a microwave oven. It was a very nice microwave oven, with a flat LED display and shiny steel interior, and were she in the market for one, this may well have been the one she'd choose.

"Are you all right?" the girl asked, blinking her mascara-lengthened lashes and affording Shaunna a smile that reflected back her own anxiety.

"Yes, I'm fine. Sorry. I'm waiting for someone, and they're late."

"Ah. OK." The girl pointed...somewhere. "I'll be over by the desk if you need any help."

Shaunna nodded. "Thank you."

As the sales assistant started to walk away, she glanced back over her shoulder and said, "The traffic's pretty bad, so whoever it is might've been held up."

Shaunna nodded again and closed the microwave door. Well, that would certainly explain it. She busied herself with examining the rest of the display, listening to Bing Crosby crooning over the store's speakers interspersed with announcements for staff to attend various departments...slowly tuning in to the conversation happening a few feet behind her.

"Accident," the young sales assistant—the one who had just spoken to Shaunna—told her colleague in hushed tones, though clearly not hushed enough. "A car jumped the lights, apparently. Police have blocked the road."

"Oh, no!" said the second sales assistant. "Is it serious?"

"I couldn't tell."

"No wonder it's so quiet this evening."

Accident.

That was the only bit Shaunna had heard. She walked off in a daze, blindly cutting through the lines of toasters, kettles, laptops, tablets…out of the doors, barely registering the bitter-cold wind whistling through the vast car park, unable to see past the bright floodlights to the street beyond other than the blue flashes of emergency vehicles, their wailed warnings setting off alarm bells in her head.

A bad accident.

She staggered onwards, across the car park and out onto the road, repeating the desperate prayer under her breath, "Please don't let it be him. Please don't let it be him." Down the street she went, the chaos of vehicles coming into view: two ambulances, several police cars; another screamed past her, leaving her temporarily deaf.

A crowd had gathered like an audience at a firework display, with their 'oohs' and 'ahhs' as they watched the emergency services quick-marching back and forth in the strobed illumination of myriad blue beacons. The cars that had crashed were beyond the barrier of people and vehicles, a dark mass but for a flickering orange indicator and a dim interior light picking out the silhouette of three people: one slumped in the left front seat, two more working frantically through the open car door.

"Left-hand drive." Shaunna gasped in terrible realisation. The nausea that hit her wasn't a battering tidal wave, more a slow-rising from her feet, gradually building momentum as it flooded up past her knees, into her abdomen, restricting her breathing as it hit her oesophagus. She made a run for the pavement, where she leaned on a garden wall, coughing and retching loudly enough to draw the attention of several of the closest rubber-necked onlookers, who sneered in disgust. She wasn't especially happy at having thrown up on her shoes either, but right now, it was the least of her concerns.

She couldn't believe she was getting in such a state when she had no idea if the car was his or not. Maybe it wasn't left-hand drive at all, and even if it was, other people owned imported cars. Generally, she was calm in a crisis, so what was this craziness about?

She spat to clear the acid from her mouth and wiped her face on her sleeve, turning back to the person closest to her. "Do you know what cars were involved?" she asked.

The person shrugged without taking their eyes from the scene. "No idea. An American car of some sort and a transit van, I think."

Shaunna felt the earth fall away beneath her feet.

***

"All right, love?" a murmured distant voice filtered through.

"Is she OK?" somebody asked.

"Yeah. Just passed out."

"I..." Shaunna found she was slumped against a garden wall, a pool of vomit a few feet away from her. She recalled it was her own, and with that recollection came everything else. "The accident..."

"Yeah," the woman said. "Nasty. Did you see it happen, love?"

Shaunna shook her head. "I...I think my friend's...the American car." Her heart was going too fast, and the nausea was threatening again.

"Ah," the woman sounded unambiguously.

"Is he...I mean, the driver..."

The woman shook her head, her face contorting in empathy. "They've taken her in the ambulance already, but..." The woman smiled gently and rubbed Shaunna's arm to offer comfort. "I'm so sorry."

"Her?" Shaunna repeated.

"Pardon?"

"The driver was a woman?"

"Of the Corvette, yes. I think it was a man driving the transit van. He was very shaken up, obviously, but otherwise, he seemed fine."

Shaunna quickly stood and swayed a little, woozy from passing out and throwing up, aware of how full her bladder *still* was—not surprising after the number of yoghurt not-smoothies she'd drunk during the afternoon. *A Corvette, not a Mustang.* Her relief, though tempered by the knowledge that the deceased driver was special to someone, was immense.

"Thank you." She smiled at the woman who had been looking after her. "I'm OK now."

She left the scene, keeping her phone in her hand all the way back to the electronics superstore, admonishing herself for overreacting. She'd been so fixated on the accident, she'd fled in a blind panic; it hadn't even crossed her mind to check the car park earlier. In fact, she'd probably walked right past him and he was still standing there, wondering why she'd gone tearing off like that.

She shook her head at her own silliness, feeling a little less frantic, and allowed her thoughts to wander ahead to planning a final Christmas shopping trip. By the time she reached the superstore, she'd calmed down considerably and was confident there would be a red Mustang parked outside, for there were still no messages on her phone.

And still no red Mustang.

"Pain in the ass," she hissed, picking up her pace as she saw her bus pass by and turn into the bus station. He'd evidently forgotten about their arrangement or decided to go and buy the rotten TV on his own, even though he'd assured her that it was *perfectly fine* with him if she wanted to meet up with Sean. If he had a problem with their friendship, why the hell didn't he say so instead of putting her through all this stress? She reached the bus and breathlessly requested a ticket, heading straight to the back, aware, after twenty-four years of parenting, that her fury was the aftereffect of the shock and worry, not that understanding why was going to stop her from ripping him to pieces.

The anger propelled her mindlessly through her journey, reducing to a simmer on the short walk to the apartments, but then reignited like a spark to a gas leak when she spotted the Mustang parked in its usual place. By the time she reached the door of his apartment, she was shaking with rage and swore profusely when the key refused to go into the lock. When it finally did go in, she twisted it hard to the right and flung the door open, storming through the lounge on a direct path to the bathroom.

"I'll talk to you in a minute," she yelled on her way past. He was sitting on the floor with his back against the sofa. That was as much as she'd taken in. She yanked down her jeans and sat on the loo, the long-awaited pee a stream that seemed to go on forever while her breath remained panting and furious.

Back in the lounge, he hadn't moved a muscle. The TV was tuned to a music channel, and the volume, she now noticed, was set too high to talk over, although the way she was feeling, he'd have absolutely no trouble hearing her. She grabbed the remote control and pressed hard on the volume button with no effect. The music wasn't coming from the TV. With a shriek, she flung the TV remote at the sofa and tried the one for his music player, this time succeeding in getting the volume down to a sensible level. She tossed that remote control at the sofa too. It bounced off the cushion and landed on the floor next to him.

"Where the hell were you?" she tried to ask quietly; her voice came out as a low, guttural growl.

"Here," he said, his eyes fixed on the screen. He turned up the music again, mouthing along to the lyrics of The Red Hot Chilli Peppers' 'Snow'. Shaunna snatched the remote control from him and switched it off.

"It's not even a bloody Christmas song!" That was totally irrelevant, but she was too angry to care.

He picked up the glass on the floor next to him and peered inside it.

"And don't pretend you forgot," she snapped, further enraged by his nonchalant glass swirling that made the ice cubes rattle.

"I didn't." He tipped the last of the vodka from the bottle into his glass.

"Andy!"

He glanced up at her but refused to meet her gaze.

"This is about Sean, isn't it?" she accused. He didn't answer. "We only meet up for a chat over a milkshake once a week. It doesn't mean—"

"No," he said, cutting her off.

"What then?"

He shrugged and emptied the glass in one go.

"And you're drinking. What the hell is the matter with you? You don't drink when we're together!"

He got up and went to the kitchen. She watched, frozen to the spot by rage and confusion. Why was he being like this? She took a few deep breaths in an attempt to calm herself and followed him.

"What's wrong?" she asked.

"I'll go get Krissi's TV tomorrow," he replied flatly.

"That's not what I'm talking about."

"Isn't it?"

She laughed in disbelief. "No! I don't care whether you buy her a stupid TV or not. I doubt she cares much either, to be quite honest."

"There you go, then." He walked past her and returned to the lounge, now with a three-quarters-full whisky bottle.

She drew up in front of him and crossed her arms. "Well?" she demanded.

"It doesn't matter what I do, does it? It makes no fucking difference."

"I'm not angry with you for not buying her a TV. I told you I never expected anything from you, and she's an adult, so it's too bloody late now, anyway. But that's beside the point. You were supposed to meet me in town and couldn't even pay me the courtesy of a text to say you weren't coming."

"Sorry."

Shaunna was set to launch again, but he looked up, straight into her eyes, and his expression instantly silenced her.

"We can't go on." His voice was quiet but firm.

"What d'you mean, we can't go on? We did all this weeks ago. I thought we were OK."

"No, we're not."

She shook her head, no idea where this had come from. "What's happened?"

"Nothing," he said. "Nothing's happened. Nothing's changed. You belong with Kris, or to Kris, whatever. So, go home to your husband, and enjoy your Christmas together."

He picked up the remote control and returned the music to its prior volume. She hesitated a moment longer, and left, slamming the door behind her.

2. Against the Rocks

H I," Kris called from the kitchen, where he was spooning sauce onto two plates of pasta.

"Hi." Shaunna paused in the doorway, taking in the pink and purple angel garland, with its coordinated twinkling lights, looped around the perimeter of the ceiling. The three of them had put up the decorations together three weeks ago, yet this evening, she felt as if she were seeing them for the first time, and they seemed tacky and out of place. Even the vanilla spice incense she had always adored was artificial and overbearing. She breathed through her mouth to block the smell and turned her attention back to Kris. "What've you got there?"

"Nothing exciting, I'm afraid. Cheese and spinach. I may have gone a little overboard on the garlic."

"Don't be coming anywhere near me!"

Kris frowned, puzzled and a little hurt. "I made it for you and me."

"Where's Ade?"

"Working. He's got one more show tonight, so he's staying at his sister's and coming back tomorrow." He set the two plates on the table and collected cutlery.

They'd been separated for more than a year, yet they still did this. They shared meals, shopping, household chores… It was normal and right and suddenly suffocating.

Kris kept his eyes trained on the cutlery, watching her in his peripheral vision and wondering why she had remained in the doorway. Before he got as far as asking, she came and sat at the table. He took the seat opposite. "How's Sean?" he asked instead.

"Fine," Shaunna replied vaguely. She spun some of the tagliatelle around her fork and blew on it.

"Is he ready for Christmas?"

"Probably not."

"And baby Dylan? How's he?"

"OK, I think."

Kris laughed, making light. "What did you talk about all afternoon?"

She shrugged. "Not a lot, really." She put the food in her mouth and chewed, struggling to swallow.

"Sorry. It's way too much garlic, isn't it? Do you want me to make something else?"

"No. It tastes good," she said. She attempted a smile, but she was fighting tears. She sniffed and forced down a second mouthful. "Any word from the lawyer?"

"Nothing." Two weeks ago, Kris had filmed his final scene as DI Mark Lundberg in the hit Anglo-Swedish crime drama *Shadows*, due to air on Christmas Day. He was waiting for his contract to be officially terminated, but he didn't want to talk about that, not when she was barely keeping it together. It wasn't like her. She was always so strong. "What's the matter?" he asked gently.

"Nothing. Just not hungry." She pushed her chair away from the table, fled from the kitchen and ran upstairs.

Kris listened to the bedroom door close behind her, straining until he was sure it was the sound of pillow-muted sobbing he could hear. He put his fork down and pinched the bridge of his nose to stop his own tears from swelling.

***

Shaunna lay on her back, staring at the ceiling, tears still trickling from the corners of her eyes. She'd heard Kris scrape the plates into the bin and felt guilty about not eating the meal he'd made for her; it was one of her favourites.

How did we come to this? She was thirty-nine years old and having an affair with the father of her illegitimate, grown-up child whilst living with her husband and his lover, and every one of them was so damned miserable. There were no secrets here… well, just the one, and she still didn't know what she was going to do about that. She was terrified what it might do to Kris after all they'd been through in the past year—the breaking up, the getting back together, the affair…

It was a crazy situation, and they'd been foolish to think it could work, to think they could live like that without anyone getting hurt, although it had worked at first. When had it all gone so horribly wrong?

The truth, she realised, now it was too late, was she wanted to be with Andy enough to tell Kris it was time they moved on. Until now, the risk of losing Kris's friendship, of the potential damage it would do to all of them and her worries for how Krissi would react, had far outweighed her feelings for Andy. Before she and Kris got together, she'd wondered what would've happened if things had been different. Maybe she and Andy would've had a fling or even had a go at a proper relationship, but they were fantasies, lived out in her head, unrealistic and impossible.

Then she'd had Krissi, and she and Kris were together, and they were happy, content. They had a good life. They loved each other. Needed each other.

But not with this burning passion, this irrepressible and desperate desire to be in his arms, to feel his body against hers.

Was it just the sex? Because the sex was good.

No. It was incredible.

What she and Kris had shared for all those years had been good too. They'd made love, watched TV, walked the dog, cooked meals. They were inseparable, in love…and she did still love him. He'd rescued her, cared for them both, given them a wonderful life, this beautiful home, given them everything, until it destroyed him. It was never about his sexuality, his 'need' to be with a man. It was about his need to be loved, to be in control. It was about Great-Uncle Anders and Krissi and Andy and all the other things Kris couldn't control.

Like Krissi being Andy's daughter.

For twenty-one years, Kris had lived with the secret, his belief that Shaunna had been raped. It would have caused him less damage if that had proved to be the truth, rather than what he now knew: that Andy was in love with her.

Not that it mattered anymore. Andy had made it clear they were over for good this time, and she could understand why. He'd hated they were having an 'affair' but told her he couldn't stop himself, and from the outset, he'd been honest about what he wanted. No more friends with benefits. He wanted to settle down and start a family.

What's with men these days?

Andy, the alpha male, wilful, irresponsible, perpetual teenager, living in the moment—it didn't exactly fit with settling down and starting a family.

In response, she'd told him she couldn't leave Kris, so she only had herself to blame. It was a bloody mess. She needed time to think. Time on her own.

Almost as if he'd read her mind, Kris shouted up to her, "I'm popping over to Dan's."

Shaunna coughed to clear her throat before she replied, hoping he wouldn't notice she'd been crying. "OK. See you later."

The front door closed, and she buried her face in the pillows.

***

Kris stood outside the apartment block, considering his options. He needed to do both, and it had to be tonight, because he wasn't sure he'd be strong enough tomorrow. *Sorry:* a straightforward, five-letter word, but the hardest one of all when it meant everything. He wondered if it would have been easier if he hadn't known the two brothers for all of living memory. There was so much history between them, even though, outside of their friendship group, they had hardly anything in common.

He called to mind some of the games of make-believe they'd played when they were little, long before any of them had developed a conscious sense of what it meant to be a boy or a girl, when it was still easy to persuade the others to put on dresses and high heels and play the role of mum, and when he didn't understand that being such an epic failure at football made him a social outcast…before his sexuality threatened to do the same.

And before the treehouse, not that he was one to seek excuses for his own atrocious behaviour, which was why, however much it hurt and whatever the consequence, he needed to say he was sorry.

Twice.

So the only decision he had to make was which brother first: Dan or Andy? He took a ten-pence piece from his pocket.

"Heads, it's Dan." He flipped the coin into the air, caught it and slapped it down on the back of his left hand, his right palm pressing against it now an immoveable object. He fought to lift his fingers and then to look down at the result of his chance decision.

Heads. His heart started hammering at the prospect of what lay ahead.

Of course, there was an easy way to do it. He could treat it like learning a script. Rehearse his lines from here to the front door and recite them with a suitably convincing veneer of remorse, sorrow…

But is that what I really feel?

The truth was, he didn't know. He'd pushed it deep, deep down, buried under all the other crap that had gone on over the years. To face it was to accept their friendship was built around his need to make amends, although Dan meant so much more to him than that. He loved him as much as he loved his own brother. Not true: he loved Dan more. Therefore, it needed to be a heartfelt apology, not varnished with melodrama that would dredge up everything else. Say sorry and leave it at that.

The door opened; he wasn't even aware he'd knocked. Adele stood before him, her hair swept up in a towel turban, an avocado-green face mask covering all but her lips and eyes. Her frown became a smile.

"Hiya," she greeted cheerily. "Come in." Kris did so. "Dan?" Adele called.

"Yep?" He appeared in the hallway. "Alright, mate? I'm just about to open a beer. You want?"

"Yeah, that'd be great, thanks." Kris followed him into the lounge. No outrageous Christmas garlands here, just a perfectly proportioned Scots pine dotted with traditional ornaments— glitter-dusted glass baubles, tiny wooden soldiers, angels, rocking horses—and flickering candle lights.

"It's beautiful," Kris said, gazing hazily past the lights into the green depths of the tree.

"Thank you." Adele kissed his cheek to acknowledge the compliment, depositing a pale creamy smear. She giggled apologetically and wiped it off with her finger. "I'm going to be rude and leave you to it," she said.

Kris could hear running water, the scent of essential oils competing with the Christmas tree. "Smells good," he said. "Have a nice bath."

"Oh, don't you worry, I intend to be in there for at least the next hour." She gave him a little wave and floated away on an aromatic cloud of steam.

Dan returned with two bottles of beer and handed one over.

"She's in a good mood," Kris observed with a nod in the direction Adele had taken.

"Yeah. We had a proper talk earlier and worked some stuff out."

"Really?" Kris was genuinely surprised because Dan and Adele didn't do proper talks. They fought and then kissed and made up.

"She wrote a letter to her mother, telling her she didn't want to see her again."

"Ooh. That's heavy."

"I won't lie, mate, it was. There's been tears shed today, I can tell you."

Hearing that didn't help Kris at all.

"So, is this just a social visit?" Dan asked.

"Kind of," he said cagily. "It sounds like you've had enough to deal with already, though, so I, err…" It would be easy to bottle out now, and with good reason rather than pathetic excuse. However, Dan was studying him and waiting for him to finish his sentence.

"I've seen that face before. When you told me what you thought happened to Shaunna at the party."

So much easier to act than do this for real. "I need to…" Kris took a swig of his beer. It was not his intent to delay. He'd rather get it over with, but his throat was suddenly dry, like when he forgot his lines on set. He realised he'd slipped into his default mode for handling difficult situations and drank some more in preparation of starting over for real.

"This is really difficult for me," he began, "but I have to say it, because I've been living with it ever since Anders…"

3. Bitters

T HE COLOUR DRAINED from Dan's face, but Kris had got this far. He had to do it now; no backing out.

Another swig of beer, another breath…

"Ever since he did what he did, I've wanted to tell you that I'm sorry, and I couldn't find the right time, or if I did find the right time I couldn't find the words, and then I'd put it off or justify it in my mind that I had nothing to say sorry for, but I—"

"Whoa!" Dan lifted his hand, his beer sloshing dangerously with the motion. "You *don't* have anything to say sorry for."

"I do, Dan. Hear me out. Don't get me wrong. I'm not saying it's my fault or anything like that, but he was my great-uncle, and I should have told my parents."

"And that would've achieved what, exactly?"

"They'd have dealt with it, stopped it from happening again after the first time. But I was a coward and chose to keep quiet."

"Mate, listen to yourself," Dan beseeched.

"You know I'm right."

"Bollocks you are! Have you heard of grooming?"

"Of course I have, but that's not what happened, is it?"

"You've got to be kidding me!"

"I could've stood up to him, Dan. But I didn't, and I've thought about it a lot since. It would've been far more damaging to you."

"Why?"

"Because you're straight."

Dan got up and started pacing, bottle in one hand, the other rubbing his head until his hair was standing on end.

Kris wished he'd never opened his mouth. He wanted to make things right for Dan, not re-open his wounds.

"That's all I wanted to say, anyway. That I'm sorry."

"And so you should be," Dan snarled, "for being a fucking idiot." He stopped pacing but remained standing because he was on the brink of losing it. He couldn't believe what he was hearing; he'd always thought Kris had dealt with what happened to them so much better than he had himself. It had taken years to come to terms with it, and he'd had Josh helping him.

He tried to keep his voice calm and quiet, hoping it would be enough to stop his anger from breaking through. "Being bisexual doesn't automatically grant someone permission to force you to do things like that."

"No, it doesn't, but the fact that I am means I wasn't made to do something I would find abhorrent."

"Oh, come on, mate! Do you think it would have fucked me up any less if he'd made me do it with a girl?"

"As a matter of fact, I do."

"Then you're fooling yourself!" Dan knocked back his beer in one go. "Have you ever talked to anyone about what happened?"

"I've told Shaunna and Ade."

"I mean a professional," Dan clarified. Kris shook his head. "D'you think it might be a good idea?"

"Why? Have you?"

"Yeah. Josh."

"So George knows too?" Kris slumped in his seat.

"Maybe, maybe not. Does it matter? We did nothing wrong."

"I don't want them all knowing about it. Does Adele know?"

"No. I can't find a way to tell her that wouldn't upset her, and that's OK, because it isn't wrecking my life anymore."

In spite of his vow to stay sober, Kris glugged heavily at his beer. Dan was right. It was wrecking his life, and he needed to talk to someone about it. For now, he'd rather deal with the fallout than defuse the bomb.

"Do you know about Shaunna and Andy?" he asked.

Dan pursed his lips. He couldn't lie, but he didn't want to admit it either. However, his reaction had answered the question.

"And do you also know Shaunna and I are still together?"

"You're joking."

"I'm not."

"I thought you broke up."

"We did."

"And that you and Ade…" Dan saw the confirmation, right there on Kris's face, but still needed to hear it in words. "You and Shaunna are still doing all the husband-and-wife bit, but you're with Ade?"

Kris nodded. He felt like a dirty pervert, no better than Anders. Dan left him alone for a moment, returning with more beer. He sat down again.

"Fuck me!" he said and started laughing at the absolute inappropriateness of his exclamation in light of what they were discussing.

"I'm a horrible person," Kris admitted, and he meant it.

"You're a bloody mess!" Dan said. "Whose idea was that? Yours?"

"No. Theirs. They kind of ganged up on me. They do it a lot, actually." Kris didn't want to get into the nitty-gritty of it, that wasn't why he was there, but equally, he wanted Dan to understand. "The thing is, when Ade and I broke things off, he accused me of pushing him away, and at the time I didn't believe him. But he's right. Even now, I'm terrified that if I leave Shaunna, I'll lose everything."

Dan shook his head in disbelief.

"Krissi is not my daughter. And I know we were friends long before everyone else came along, but Ellie, Jess and I were only ever on the periphery. It's always been the six of you, from St. Mark's—I hadn't realised until we were at Cordelia's Aquarium the other week, but it's like you all made a childhood pact to stand by each other. And it was there at George and Josh's wedding too—I guess it's always been there, but it's more pronounced when Cordelia's around."

"Only because she was our teacher for two bloody long years."

"And cast some kind of magic friendship spell on you?"

In spite of the matter at hand, Kris's comment made Dan chuckle. Cordelia Kinkade was a very traditional primary school teacher who would gush with praise if it was deserved or come down on a kid like a screeching ton of bricks if they stepped out of line. Dan had been one of those kids who was rarely in line to begin with, like his older brothers. So while Mrs. Kinkade might have been the favourite teacher of super-swots like Josh, Dan had thought she was an evil witch. Of course, as an adult, he could appreciate what a bloody nuisance he'd been. He had to admit it had been good to see her again after all those years, especially as these days, he was friends with the teacher's pet.

"All I'm saying," Kris continued, bringing Dan's thoughts back to the present, "is that the six of you will always be friends, whatever happens. Us three on the outside? Well, Ellie only made it because she was Josh's best friend in high school, Jess because she was with Andy, and me because—"

"Of Shaunna?"

Kris shrugged. "Or you. Either way, I'm an outsider, and doing the right thing by Shaunna and Ade..." Kris didn't finish. He couldn't stand the thought of losing his friends, but he couldn't see it ending any other way, and what choice did he have? "So that's why I had to say sorry about Anders."

Dan was troubled by what he was hearing. "You're not, err... gonna do something drastic, are you, mate?"

Kris was mortified by the suggestion. "God, no. Or no more drastic than this. I want to make things right. You're my oldest friend and, soppy as it is to say so, I love you. The prospect of losing you..."

Dan rubbed his eyes, trying to get his head around what Kris was telling him, because it wasn't just Kris who was feeling like this. In the past year, their entire friendship group had been forced to face up to the fragility of life more than once, and it had changed them all.

Dan remained silent for several minutes, thinking and frowning. He gulped the last of his beer and went to the kitchen for two more.

"You know me," he said when he returned, "I'm all about systems and how they work."

Kris nodded, although he wasn't sure how it was relevant to the context.

"Well, I've thought about this a few times since Tom christened us The Circle, and while I take your point about us lot from St. Mark's, Tom's spot on. See, you can put any one of us in the centre and connect the rest of us to that hub."

Kris got ready to argue to the contrary, but Dan talked over him.

"And the way I see it, you're the most stable hub we've got. Put you at the centre, and there we all are. On one spoke, it's me, Andy and Adele. On another, it's George, Josh, Ellie and Jess. And on the other, Shaunna and Krissi, and then there's Ade. D'you see what I'm getting at?"

"And Sean?"

"He's Josh's mate, which—"

"And Shaunna's."

"Is he?"

"Yep. They meet up at Milky's every week."

"Hm. Well, there's something I didn't know. But regardless, it still comes back to you. You aren't just an extension. You're pivotal. The pivot." Dan frowned. "Sorry, mate. It sounds like a rude name—*you pivot*!" He started chuckling to himself.

"No, your model's all wrong," Kris slurred, realigning their friends in the imaginary and somewhat blurry wheel in his mind's eye. So much for staying sober. He set his half-full bottle on the table and pointed at it. "That's Shaunna at the centre." He swooshed his arm around in a circular motion, catching the neck of the bottle with his sleeve.

Dan scooped the bottle out of harm's way. "Eyyy!" He grinned.

"Eyyy!" Kris snatched the bottle back and kept hold of it. "So, Shaunna in the middle, and then it's me and Krissi, then Adele and you, then Andy and Jess, then…" Kris stopped and frowned, his thoughts befuddled.

Dan nodded superciliously. "See? You can't comfortably fit George and Josh in that formation."

"I can!"

"Nope." Dan refused to entertain aloud the notion that Shaunna was central to their friendship group, although he completely agreed. Shaunna's high school pregnancy had brought the nine of them together and forced her to set down roots when the rest of them were free to roam, but without Kris, she would not have become the strong, confident, beautiful woman she was; their bedrock; the home they all returned to.

They'd both finished their beers again. Dan went and got more. "There you go, you pivot." He had the giggles. Kris ignored him.

"I still say it's Shaunna."

"Wrong."

"You know it's true."

"Look, mate, I'm not trying to get one up on you, but I've already been through what you're going through now, and when you're feeling shit about yourself, you think everyone else sees you that way as well. I'm pretty sure I speak for all of us when I say we want you to be happy, whether that's with Shaunna or with Ade or both. Well, Andy might not agree on the both bit."

"He knows."

Dan raised an eyebrow. "That's between the two of you to sort out. Whatever, we'll still be mates."

"But he's your brother," Kris countered.

"That doesn't mean I'm gonna take his side."

"You're talking shit."

"How would you know? You're pissed, Johansson!" Dan hadn't mentioned that he'd already drunk four bottles before Kris arrived, and Kris rarely drank, so they were both in a similarly inebriated state.

"I'm not!"

"You bloody well are. But anyway, shut up and listen a sec." Dan could hear the bath draining and wanted to reiterate what he'd already said. "Back in primary school, I was a proper little ruffian, always defying authority, as you know. I was a tough kid. I had to be with two older brothers always trying to knock seven shades out of me. And like you, I thought I should've been the one to stand up for us because that scumbag was your uncle. But as Josh pointed out, it doesn't matter how tough you are in that situation. It's the psychological stuff that makes you weak—the grooming. Neither of us could've stopped it. That's what you've got to accept. You owe me nothing."

"But still—"

"Don't you dare. We're mates. Whether you're with Shaunna, Ade or doing some other weird swinging shit, we're mates. That's all there is to it."

"It's not swinging," Kris protested.

Adele appeared in the doorway, minus the turban and face mask, and wrapped in a fluffy pink towel. "What's not swinging?" she asked.

Kris leaned closer to Dan. "Although I could be persuaded," he joked, eyeing Adele over. In reality, he wouldn't dream of it, even if her skin was glowing, the towel draped perfectly over her breasts, around her hips—she'd have been enough of a temptress if they'd both been sober, and they were far from it.

"I'm going," Kris said. It took him a couple of attempts to get up, and he staggered a little once he was on his feet. He would have to leave Andy until tomorrow, but he wasn't worried about being able to see it through anymore. Whether Dan was right or wrong, Kris accepted that their friendship was as solid as ever.

"I'll see you out," Dan said, following him across the lounge.

"Night, Adele," Kris waved approximately in her direction.

"Night," she replied. She noticed all the beer bottles and tutted.

Kris stopped at the front door, and he and Dan embraced.

"You take it easy, all right?" Dan said.

Kris nodded. "I will. I'm going to talk to someone. A professional, like you said."

"Good idea."

"Yeah." Kris turned to walk away but then turned back. "Can I just say one thing, though?"

"Does it involve the word 'sorry'?"

"Well…"

"No. Fuck off." Dan shut the door and put his knee against the letterbox. Kris pushed on it from the outside; it resisted. Dan laughed.

"Bastard," Kris said, also laughing, as he drunkenly began to meander his way home.

Dan turned back to Adele. She was standing in the centre of the hallway, directly under a sprig of mistletoe. She glanced up and, with a sultry smile, slowly released the towel.

4. Seeing Red

ANDY STIRRED AND rolled onto his side, squashing his nose against the back rest. He licked his lips and swallowed, first registering the dreadful taste of last night's spirit cocktail, and then his location.

"Ugh!" he groaned. "Sofa."

The memory of why he was asleep on the sofa rather than in his warm, comfortable, king-size bed returned a second later, along with an armful of pins and needles. He rolled over again and opened one eye. The TV was muted, the colour and motion painfully vivid on a dark winter's morning, especially after a late night of solitary drinking. He felt like shit and it wasn't just the alcohol. What was he thinking? *Oblivion. That's right.* He wondered how long it would take him to get to the point where he could stomach another drink, because it had to beat feeling like this. Not that the bottle was his usual choice of solace; the gym or a road trip, or in the past something even more adventurous had been his style.

His cramped style. *Bloody women.*

He almost laughed out loud at the thought, although it was his brother's voice he heard, not his own. Andy wasn't like that. He was more the worship-and-adore sort, which wasn't a vast improvement for either camp, and he *had* curtailed his wayward ways for women in the past. His mother and Jess, that is. Shaunna had never asked that of him and never would, but it didn't matter anymore. It was over.

He pulled a cushion on top of his face and pushed all of his breath into it with a deep, heavy sigh. It was over, and it hurt like hell.

The doorbell rang, a viciously loud *ding-dong* in spite of the muffling effect of the cushion.

"No-one's home," he said, pulling the padding down over his ears.

Ding-dong.

"Go away!"

Ding-dong.

"Fuck off!"

Ding-dong.

"For Christ's sake." Andy chucked the cushion across the room and got up. "Oh, Jesus." He grabbed his head, vowing to get his cursing under control. Being this hungover didn't excuse his appalling language, although the comedy value of opening the door to find an outraged Jehovah's Witness standing there wasn't entirely lost on him, and he smiled to himself as he turned the lock. That smile disappeared in an instant when he saw who was actually standing outside.

"Hello, Andy," Kris greeted quietly.

"What're you doing here?"

"Can we talk?"

"Didn't you say all you needed to yesterday?"

"What I said yesterday..." Kris averted his eyes. He didn't want to do this on the doorstep. "Can I come in? Please?"

Andy moved aside.

Kris nodded in thanks and stepped into the hallway, waiting for Andy to close the door. He followed him through to the spacious lounge and glanced around at the minimal furnishings: a TV, music system, illuminated red and cream branches in a tall vase, the big red sofa, the empty bottles lying on the carpet...

"You might as well get it over with," Andy said, flopping down heavily onto the sofa.

"Get what over with?"

"Kill me. Because if she's feeling even a tenth as bad as I am..."

Kris understood now. "I didn't mean it as a threat," he said.

"That's what it sounded like. 'If you hurt her, I'll kill you'?"

"And you have hurt her."

"I know." Owning up didn't make Andy feel any better about it. "She won't leave you, Kris. She loves you."

"Yeah, she does. Because I looked after her."

"Saved her from me."

"Kept her from you. That's what you mean."

"No." Andy shook his head—not a wise idea. He winced and continued. "After you'd gone yesterday, I thought about coming after you, beating the shit out of you for all you've put me through—telling Dan I raped her, then attacking him, thinking it was me. I wanted to rip you apart with my bare hands."

"I was wrong," Kris admitted. "About everything."

"That's just it. You weren't. You love Shaunna and Krissi, and I admire what you've done for them. I'm so bloody jealous of what you've got, and that's not who I am. A jealous guy."

"Why wouldn't you be jealous? You love her, don't you?"

"You've no idea." Andy slapped his palms over his eyes. He could feel tears prickling, and there was no way he was going to cry. Not in front of Kris.

"Can I make you a drink or something?" Kris offered. Andy laughed behind his hands.

"No," he said, dragging himself to his feet. "I'll do it. Tea or coffee?"

"Coffee, thanks."

Andy wandered off across the room. "Sit down," he called back.

Kris perched at one end of the sofa, trying to keep at bay the noxious thought of how many times Shaunna and Andy had screwed on this very spot. It no longer made him angry, or not with them; with himself, for trying to keep them apart. Andy returned and collected the empty spirit bottles.

"You got hammered last night," Kris stated.

"Yeah," Andy confirmed. "Feeling it this morning." He took the bottles away.

"Me and Dan had a few beers."

"Did you?"

"Yeah."

It was a shouted conversation across the expanse of the enormous lounge, but a conversation, nonetheless.

"You don't drink," Andy said.

"No. Neither do you, much."

Andy returned with the coffees and passed one to Kris. "You remember why when you wake up the morning after."

Kris smiled. "Don't I know it."

Andy sat at the other end of the sofa, which was big enough that neither was invading the other's space, although there was a lot more that needed to be said to clear the air between them. The confrontation the previous afternoon had been coming for months, and whilst neither wanted to blame the other, nor did they wish to take sole responsibility.

"I wanted to intimidate you," Kris admitted.

"Yeah. I got that."

"I know you're straight really."

Andy raised an eyebrow and shifted uncomfortably.

"And you're a good-looking guy, but you and Dan are like brothers to me."

"So it's OK to have a three-way relationship with Ade and Shaunna, but you wouldn't sleep with someone you see as a brother?"

"What can I say? I'm a fuck-up."

Andy laughed dryly. "I'm kind of flattered, if I'm honest."

That didn't ease Kris's embarrassment. Trying to make light of it, he said, "Well, you're safe, I promise you. You're actually

not the sort of guy I usually fall for, but that is one hell of a…
fear response."

"Yeah, tell me about it," Andy grumbled. Danger excited him,
a little too much.

"I really do love Ade."

"And Shaunna?"

"I love her too. There's so much that's happened in the last
couple of years, I couldn't get my head together enough to think
clearly about how I felt. I couldn't accept it was over between us,
but I knew when the paternity tests came back. I was a reserve
playing in a match I wasn't ready for."

Andy gave Kris a dubious look. "Great football analogy, mate,
but total bollocks. Without you, Shaunna would've been a single
mum in a council flat, struggling to make ends meet. Krissi is
the woman she is today because *you* are her dad, not me. You're
selling yourself short."

"I owe you an apology…"

"Maybe you do, but don't insult Krissi or Shaunna by
regretting standing by them all these years."

That stung, and it took Kris quite a time to recover. He sat
quietly, sipping his coffee and mulling over Andy's words. Even
if he hadn't come here this morning to say he was sorry and tell
Andy he was ready to stand aside so that Shaunna was free, that
statement alone stood as confirmation that it was the right thing
to do.

"I still owe you an apology," he said. "You and everyone else,
for my utter stupidity in thinking that breaking up with Shaunna
would end our friendship."

"That *is* fucking stupid," Andy agreed.

"Yeah. Dan put me straight last night. Kind of. We were both
a bit too pissed for it to make any sense, but I've been awake since
four, and I've thought about it long and hard." Kris registered the
innuendo and blushed.

Andy laughed and patted him on the thigh. "Kris, mate…"

"Yeah, I know. I was being greedy."

Andy was still laughing. "That's not what I meant."

"It's true enough," Kris said humbly. "I was trying to have everything."

"You hear that a lot?" Andy asked. "The whole 'bisexuals are greedy' bull?"

"All the time. It's that or 'there's no such thing'. It makes me so angry, but I can't show it in public. Got to be the great ambassador."

Andy had heard it before, from Charlie. She was a semi-pro footballer, and whilst they'd only become friends in the last year, they'd known each other since Charlie got picked up by the England squad at the age of sixteen, making her the envy of boys and girls alike. She'd forever had to fight the stereotypical assumption that woman footballer equals lesbian, and that made it harder still to tell people she was bi.

But unlike Kris, Charlie wasn't in the limelight, so she did at least get to vent her frustrations when people accused her of being confused or trying to blend in or, as Kris said, being greedy. Andy could personally testify to the fact that falling in love wasn't a choice, or else he and Kris wouldn't be trying to fix their friendship because of Shaunna. He could only imagine how much more complicated it would be in the face of all that bigotry. Relationships were tough enough already.

"I don't feel up to the task," Kris said, cutting through Andy's thoughts.

"Of?"

"Being the bisexual ambassador, not when I'm making such a cock-up of..." This time he laughed at the double entendre himself. Andy joined in for a little while, and then they both became quiet and thoughtful again.

"There's nothing wrong with wanting everything," Andy said philosophically. "We all do it. I remember once, spelunking in the Philippines—"

"What-ing?"

"Exploring caves. This cavern was enormous and the rock formations were like something from another world. And I kept thinking how awesome it was to be there, yet wishing I had someone to go home to and share it with. But there was no way I would've given it up for love, and when I had to, it made me miserable. I miss the adventure and I want to have both."

"You can have both," Kris reasoned. "It's not the same, is it? Going splunking, or whatever it's called, and being in a relationship aren't mutually exclusive."

"And so can you."

"How?"

"You weren't after two intimate relationships. You wanted to be with Ade and keep your daughter and friends, and they're not mutually exclusive, either."

"I know. I get that now. And I am going to fix it, somehow. But you can't give up who you are for someone else."

"Yeah, well, who's gonna put up with me buggering off to go boarding whenever the urge takes me?"

"Shaunna would."

"That doesn't make it right."

"So take her with you."

"Are you serious?"

"Absolutely." Kris sat forward so he could properly make eye contact with Andy. "Look, we both know she's her own person, and me doing the right thing won't guarantee she'll want to make a go of it with you. She sacrificed everything for Krissi, and, I'm sorry to say, for me. If you're going to do this, then for God's sake, make it work for both of you. You deserve each other."

Andy had just taken a mouthful of coffee and choked on it. "I'm not sure how to take that," he spluttered.

"I mean you both deserve to be happy. And I'm truly sorry I got in the way of that."

They maintained the eye contact a little longer, and then Andy nodded.

"Cheers. That means a lot. I'm sorry too."

"For?"

"Having an affair with your wife."

"It wasn't really, was it? And, like I say, she makes up her own mind. She told me, when I accused her, that you both tried not to but couldn't help it, which I totally understand. Anyway, I think if you get yourself spruced up a bit, we could maybe go back to the house and sort this mess out."

"Spruced up?"

"You smell like a drunk. In fact, you look like a drunk. You slept in your clothes."

"Yeah. On the sofa."

Kris shuddered.

"Freak," Andy said, retreating to the bathroom. "And anyway, it's my bloody sofa. I'll sleep on it if I damn well want to!"

5. Rekindled Flame

KRIS PUT HIS key in the lock and turned back to check on Andy. "You OK?"

"No. I'm crapping myself."

Kris pushed the door open. Andy held his breath.

"Kris?" Shaunna's voice called from upstairs.

"Yeah."

"Where've you been? Ade came back. He said you were supposed to be going shopping."

"We are. I had to sort something out. I found this drunkard who'd slept in his clothes and brought him home with me for a cup of tea."

"You did wh—" Shaunna stopped halfway down the stairs, her hair scooped in her hand ready to be tied back, but she hadn't got that far. It took her a few seconds to release it.

"Hi," Andy said, trying to keep his voice steady.

Shaunna looked from Andy to Kris in confusion.

"You two need to talk," Kris said. "Where's Ade? Upstairs?"

Shaunna nodded dumbly. Kris moved off, passing her on the stairs. She searched his face for an explanation. He smiled, and that smile was everything—apology, love, humility. Everything.

"Go talk to Andy. We'll deal with us later."

He continued on his way, leaving her standing, still with one foot up and one foot down.

She turned her attention back to Andy, and they both listened to Ade laying into Kris for making him come back from Manchester in rush hour when he wasn't even home.

Shaunna found she could move her legs again and made it to the bottom of the stairs. She stopped in front of Andy, who hadn't moved a muscle since he crossed the Johansson threshold. He was freshly showered and shaved, his dark hair a tousled mess, just how she liked it. She felt a shiver of desire run through her.

"Drunkard?" she queried.

"Yeah," Andy admitted guiltily. "I finished off the whisky, then started on the gin."

"Blimey. Bet you're suffering now."

"A bit," he confirmed, though the hangover was nothing by comparison. She took a step closer to him. He stood his ground.

"I'm still angry with you," she said.

"Fair enough."

"There was an accident. An American car jumped the lights. The driver died."

"Shit." Andy closed his eyes. It was both an instinctive response to the tragic news and a means of holding on to his wavering self-control. He could feel the heat radiating from her body, hot spots forming on his torso corresponding to her breasts. He inhaled the scent of her shampoo, so familiar to him now that he could imagine too well how it would feel to comb his fingers through her hair, take her in his arms and—

"I thought it was you."

The spell temporarily broken, he opened his eyes again to find she'd advanced on him further, her face now only a couple of inches from his.

"I'm really sorry." He was so desperate to hold her he had to ball his fists to stop himself.

"Yeah, well, so you should be." She stretched up on tiptoes so that she was closer still. "I'll go and put the kettle on," she murmured huskily, her breath making his skin tingle. Her lips grazed his.

A door opened, and Kris and Ade's voices floated down the stairs ahead of them. Shaunna slowly backed off.

"We're going now," Kris said. "See you in a couple of hours."

"A couple of hours? You're optimistic!"

"I've only got one present left to buy, and Ade's all done."

"God, I wish I was that organised," Andy grumbled.

"Yeah, same here," Shaunna agreed. They moved out of the way to let Kris and Ade pass.

Ade gave Shaunna a hug. "Be nice," he whispered in her ear. She shoved him away and glared at him. He winked in response. "See you later." He followed Kris out of the door.

Andy glanced over his shoulder to watch them leave. The second the door shut, Shaunna pushed up against him, steering him backwards until he was pinned against it, and flicked the snip on the lock. She stretched up on sock-covered toes to reach him, pressing her mouth hard against his. He responded by playfully biting her lip while trying to extract himself from the kiss.

"We can't do this here," he pleaded breathlessly.

"Why not? We're home alone."

"But this is yours and Kris's house. It's not right."

"Oh, to hell with you and your 'it's not right'!" She pulled the end of his belt free of its buckle, and he writhed uncontrollably against her.

"Don't!" he gasped, but it was as much protest as he could muster, as she had already unzipped his jeans and was now slowly dropping to her knees, her breasts brushing against him on the way down. Even though they were both fully clothed, it rendered him helpless, and all he could think about was how much he wanted to slide down the straps of that lacy bra he had caught a tantalising glimpse of as she went down.

For about two seconds, he successfully fought the urge to touch her hair and then gave up, spiralling the fiery curls around his fingers, gently guiding her movements, pushing forward as she did.

She ran her hands up his thighs and around his hips, grasping at his denim-clad buttocks, pulling him closer and deeper, loving the sound of his groans, the increased tension in his muscles, the intensity of his thrusts. She wanted him, and it was making her ache and throb. Her hips moved without her conscious control as her body sought contact, yearning for release. And yet she held off, enjoying the taste of him, his response to her, the animal need that diminished his resistance.

She slowed down to give them both longer, using her tongue instead of her mouth until he regained some control, and then she took him once more, sucking hard, digging her fingers in so he couldn't escape, squeezing tighter, taking him deeper as he began thrusting again, harder and faster than before.

He tried to pull away, but she kept hold of him and continued to move with him as he shuddered and climaxed, steadying himself with a hand against the wall. She stayed where she was, smiling around him, delighting in the pulsing against her tongue and the breathless, jelly-legged mess she had made of him, the simple fact of his presence. He was here. It wasn't over. She slowly pulled herself upright. His other hand was still tangled in her hair, and he used it to steer her mouth up to meet his. She kissed him gently.

"What about you?" Andy asked, inhaling his own scent.

"There's time for that later." Shaunna eased him back inside his jeans and re-zipped them. "Let's go talk." Taking him by the hand, she led him to the kitchen and pointed at a chair. "Sit," she instructed.

He did so, not that he had much choice. He was still wobbly in the aftermath and struggling to bear his own weight.

She filled the kettle and prepared two mugs before turning to face him. "You look shocked," she said.

"Yeah. It's been a really weird morning. D'you ever think you might still be asleep and it's all a dream?"

She laughed. "Why?"

"Your husband threatens me one day, the next, he's hanging on my doorbell at the crack of dawn, saying he's sorry and ordering me to come and talk to you. Then he has the bloody cheek to nag me all the way here about sleeping on my own sofa."

"And that's the bit that makes you think you're dreaming?"

"Well…" Andy grinned coyly. He stood up, legs still a little shaky, and wrapped his arms around her, planting a kiss in her hair. "What you just did was pretty unbelievable too."

"That good, was it?"

"I mean, I can't believe you did it in the hallway of your family home where you've lived with your husband all these years and raised your daughter. How many times has Krissi come running in and out of that door?"

"The ghosts of Christmas past," Shaunna tormented. "You didn't enjoy it?"

"It still doesn't feel right doing it here, but yeah. It was awesome."

She tweaked his nose and turned away to make the tea. "I'm pleased to hear it."

When she was done, she passed him his mug and ushered him back to the table, where she sat and shuffled her chair until she was sitting with her legs between his. He was staring down at her knees, and she grabbed his hands and shook them to make him look up. "Is that why you finished things yesterday?" she asked. "Because of Kris?"

Andy nodded. "He came to see me, and I got myself all, err…" He coughed and blushed. Shaunna giggled. "It's not funny," he complained.

"Sorry."

He raised an eyebrow, not believing she was sorry for one minute. She leaned forward and kissed him. "He made a big deal out of it."

"It *is* a big deal." Shaunna grinned.

"Stop it!" Andy chastised, although he was laughing too, and still blushing. "I think he's got me down as some kind of Casanova."

"If the cap fits…"

Andy withdrew and picked up his tea.

"Sorry," she said again. She did mean it this time. "I know you're not."

"No. I'm not. I told you. I waited a long time for you. I love you."

"I still reckon it's my hair rather than me."

Andy huffed and said nothing. He was used to her deflecting, but it didn't stop him from hoping.

"So how did he threaten you, exactly?"

"He says he didn't mean it as a threat, but he told me he'd kill me if I hurt you, and I don't doubt he would."

"And what's the first thing you do? Dump me and leave me stranded in an electronics superstore, freaking out that you've had an accident."

"Yeah. Sorry about that."

"They tried to sell me a microwave."

"They've got a nerve," Andy said, playing along.

"It was a really nice one too," she said. "But it's OK. I didn't fall for their sales tricks." She gave him a feeble smile. The accident had shaken her up pretty badly.

"You didn't really freak out, did you?"

"I threw up and passed out. Does that count?"

"No shit!"

"And that's not me, you know? Level-headed all the way." Shaunna made light of it because it was absolutely not like her to panic the way she had. She'd been led to believe she was one of those people who could be relied on to stay calm in a crisis. So, along with the shock of the accident and then being dumped, she felt a bit out of sorts: emotional and vulnerable. "I thought I'd never see you again, and I couldn't deal with it," she admitted.

"But you still won't tell me you love me."

"I threw up and passed out because I thought I'd never see you again. How obvious do I need to make it?"

"Yeah, OK." Andy took her hand in his, circling his thumb over the smooth skin. "It is more than just the sex, isn't it?"

"Do you really need to ask?"

"Yeah, I do. I mean, the sex is…"

"Hot?" she prompted.

"Hell, yes! And so are you, my red-hot baby, but if that's all there is? Kris has a point."

"You don't honestly believe that?"

"He's prepared to walk away from his life with you, to risk losing Krissi and his friends, for us."

"He's got Ade."

"I know, but can you live with it? If that's all he's left with and this thing between us turns out to be nothing more than lust?"

"It won't come to that," Shaunna said with certainty. "He's being paranoid, and he can be very persuasive. I speak from experience."

Andy sighed in exasperation. She was avoiding answering his question, and it bothered him. Even if she was right and he had merely been sucked in by Kris's paranoia, he wanted reassurance that she felt the same for him as he did for her. He couldn't live with the guilt of what it might do to Kris to find out he'd given up everything for nothing more than a brief, passionate fling. More than that, he wasn't sure he could live without her. He could feel her eyes burning into him and looked up.

"You remember what you told me?" she asked. "About living in the moment and enjoying it while we're together?"

He nodded.

"Let's do that, shall we?" He looked away. "Andy?" She shuffled closer, but still he wouldn't look at her. She got up and straddled him, lifting his chin with her finger, flicking her tongue up the cleft and probing inside his mouth. He let her in, meeting the pressure of her lips. She felt him becoming aroused and slid closer, pushing her breasts against his chest. He tried to back off, but she put her hands behind his head.

"Nuh-uh," she sounded, slowly moving against him. He ran his palms up her back, her top rising with them. She wriggled her arms free and removed it.

"I still don't like this," he said between the kisses, but now she'd unfastened her bra and his self-control dropped to the floor with it. She tugged at his T-shirt, and he leaned forward so she could remove that too. "What if they come home?" he asked, the last word melting into a groan as her naked breasts squashed warm and soft against his bare chest.

"They won't," she assured him, kissing and nipping at his lips. "Not yet. And the snip's on." She got up and removed her leggings and knickers.

"Or if Krissi comes round?"

"She's at work."

She unzipped his jeans and pushed the waistband down, easing it over his hips. He lifted from the chair to make it easier. There was no point fighting her. She was going to seduce him. Again. And in that moment, he realised that if this really was all she had to offer, he'd take it.

6. Goodwill

W HAT'S WITH YOU today, sweedie?" Shaunna's boss, Hayley, watched her drift past in a daydream.

"Hmm?"

"Did the wind bleau and make that liddle smile stick?"

Shaunna blushed and giggled. "I'm just looking forward to Christmas, Hayles. That's all. How about you?"

"Well, you know, sweedie, Marvin's planned a special liddle treat for me, but he's giving nothing away. I just might have to try and tease it out of him at the Tradesman's Ball later."

Shaunna quickly pushed away the image that had popped into her mind of Hayley 'teasing' her pudgy little plumber husband and said, "If you like, I'll close up today, so you can relax while you get ready."

"You don't mind?"

"Not at all. It's the least I can do after all you've done for me this past year."

Hayley gave Shaunna a light hug, touched by her offer and her gratitude. Shaunna was an excellent stylist and had a wonderful way with the customers, even the more difficult ones, so it was worth Hayley's while to make sure she was happy in her work. During the past few months, when Shaunna had needed time off, her regulars had postponed their appointments until she returned. Thus, Hayley's kindness was partly business sense, but she also considered Shaunna to be a good friend, and she wouldn't take advantage. It was going to be a busy day, and Hayley was still uncertain about accepting the offer.

Shaunna gave her a nod and a smile of reassurance. "It's fine, Hayles, really."

"If you're definitely sure, then…" Shaunna tutted and rolled her eyes in exasperation. Hayley hugged her again. "That'd be fab, thanks, sweedie." A loud snore sounded from across the salon. Both women glanced over at Mrs. Armitage, fast asleep under the dryer. The magazine slipped from her lap to the floor. "How long's she been under?"

Shaunna shrugged. "No idea. You put her there."

"I'll ged a fork. See if she's cooked," Hayley joked and headed off into the stockroom behind the shop.

Shaunna checked the time. The morning was going slowly, with a few cancellations because of the snow, but this afternoon, there was a hen party coming in, which would be great fun if the others they'd done were any indication, and the time would fly by. She'd yet to decide whether that was a good thing and was trying not to dwell on it too much. The shop doorbell tinkled, and she turned to see who it was, setting the butterflies flapping like they were trying to break free.

"Good morning, RHB." Andy advanced with a smile, took Shaunna in his arms and kissed her, open-mouthed and passionate, only releasing her when Hayley came back. She eyed Andy appreciatively and wiggled her eyebrows up and down a couple of times.

"I think I know what made that liddle smile stick, sweedie," she said. She waved a fork at Shaunna and clicked her teeth saucily.

Andy looked from one to the other of the two women in bemusement. Hayley advanced on Mrs. Armitage, brandishing the fork as if she really was intending to prod her with it, until Shaunna gasped and covered her mouth with her hand. Hayley laughed and put the fork away, instead switching off the dryer. The sudden end to the noise brought Mrs. Armitage to her senses.

"OK, sweedie?" Hayley asked in the sickly sweet tone she reserved for customers. "Led me check those curlers for you."

Shaunna turned her attention back to Andy. "I only left your place three hours ago. Have you got nothing better to do than stalk me?"

"Nope. Dan told me to have the day off."

"Is that so?"

"Yeah. I had a few things to sort out."

"OK. Well, I'm here until five thirty, at least."

"Oh." Andy looked disappointed. "I guess I could go to the gym. Or maybe I'll sit outside in the car, stalk you from there."

"You know, sweedie?" Hayley called over, having been eavesdropping the whole time. "If you fancy a liddle freelance work, I could sure pud those beaudiful muscles to good use."

Shaunna burst out laughing.

"Doing what?" Andy asked.

"Hen party," Shaunna explained. "By the way, this is Hayley, my boss. Hayles, this is Andy, my—boyfriend?"

She glanced up at Andy as she said it, and he suddenly found he couldn't shift the smile from his face. Despite the presence of the other two women, he put his arms around Shaunna from behind and nuzzled her neck.

"Boyfriend?" he repeated. "I can most definitely go with that!"

"So whad'ya say?" Hayley prompted. "About the hen party?"

"How's it work?"

"Champagne, facials, acrylic nails, cud and blow. It's tons of fun."

"How many?"

"Six."

Andy freed one hand and rubbed his chin thoughtfully. "Hmm. Spend the afternoon with eight gorgeous women or go for a workout?"

Hayley fluttered her eyelashes at the compliment, although with the beautician and manicurist, there would be ten of them.

"Damn," Shaunna said, "wish I was free to come with you."

Andy shook his head in mock despair. "OK, tell you what," he suggested to Hayley, "I'll go do what I need to and come back for three."

"Really, sweedie?"

"If you're serious about it, yeah. Why not?"

"Oh, I'm always serious about business," Hayley said, and it was absolutely true. Her salon was small and modest compared to the big chain-owned salons in the town centre, and she had a steady clientele of older women. Gimmicks like the hen parties made good money and brought new custom in the longer term. Having a hunk around to entertain the ladies was, to her, the perfect sexy icing on the cake.

"So what d'you want me to do? Serve hors d'oeuvres in a G-string?" He was joking, although Hayley's face lit up like a Christmas tree. Shaunna shot her a warning glance and elbowed Andy in the abs.

Hayley thought for a moment and clicked her fingers. A brainwave had hit. "Construction gear," she said. "Do you own a hard hat, big boots, all that jazz?"

"I might be able to pull it together." Andy grinned. He had a cupboard full of the real deal.

"Fab, sweedie. You can be tinkering with the dryers, gedding all hod and bothered, maybe take off your top and give us all a liddle flash of those sweat-sheened pecs."

"Sure," Andy agreed.

"Oh my god!" Shaunna's mouth dropped open. "I can't believe you're actually going to do this!"

Andy kissed her again and released her. "Best go wax my bikini line," he said with a wink. "See you at three."

"Ba-bye now," Hayley called cheerily, giving him a little wave as he departed. Shaunna was still gawping in shock.

"Well," Hayley said, "if you can't fix me up with that lovely Irish psychiadrist pal of yours, then at least you can led me take a peek-a-boo at your B-F. Does he have a brother?"

"He has two," Shaunna replied, wondering why on earth she was telling her that.

"Fancy! Are they as hod as Andy?"

Shaunna didn't answer that one. All three Jeffries brothers were the same height and build, but Mike lacked Andy and Dan's charm and charisma, which made him seem less attractive, although that was more to do with his attitude problem. Still, she'd met Hayley's husband and didn't imagine Hayley would be too fussy about the personality side of things, so maybe it was better to keep quiet or else she'd have them doing a *Full Monty* style strip routine.

***

"Hi," Kris called as he closed the front door. "Brr. It is free-ee-zing out there."

Casper came racing from the kitchen, tail wagging so hard it was spinning like a helicopter rotor-blade. He delivered his gift of a freshly laundered tea towel into Kris's waiting hand. Kris reached into his jacket pocket and pulled out a paper bag. "What's this?" he said in a baby-talk voice, making the dog even more excited. "Is it a present for Caspy?" He squeezed the bag, and the thing inside squeaked. Casper went scurrying around in circles and seesawed up and down.

Josh appeared at the kitchen door. "Hey, Kris," he greeted. He was working at Kris and Shaunna's because the glazier was at his and George's place, racing to finish the double glazing before Christmas. Given that it was the twenty-third of December and there were three inches of snow on the ground, it was something of a tall order.

"Sit," Kris commanded Casper. The dog just about managed to get his bottom on the floor, his tail still swishing frantically.

Kris extracted the Christmas pudding squeaky toy from the paper bag and held it in front of the golden Labrador's snout. He sniffed at the toy for a while, checking it out thoroughly before he took it and plodded off to his bed where he lay down and stared at it, waiting for it to squeak. Josh thought it highly amusing.

"It'll take him a while to figure out how it works," Kris said. "Not like your Blue."

"Oh, Casper doesn't do so badly," Josh defended.

"For a dippy blonde."

Josh scowled. "Hey! Us blondes don't like being stereotyped." His complaint was only partly in jest. Being a psychologist meant he could be very outspoken on such matters, although on this occasion, a squeak from the Christmas pudding made his point for him. "See?" he said. "Not so dippy after all!"

"I guess not," Kris agreed. "Right. I'll get that kettle on. Coffee?"

"Wonderful."

Kris went through to the kitchen. "You know you're welcome to help yourself, don't you?"

"I do, thank you. I have had a couple, but I don't want to take advantage when you've let me stay here and you're all out at work."

"That's what friends are for," Kris said, then groaned at the cliché.

Josh smiled. "It's true enough."

"Well, I'm finished now till New Year's Eve. I have to say, the interview I've just done was the strangest yet. No questions about Shaunna or Ade or why I quit *Shadows*."

"Maybe the TV network lawyers warned them about you in advance."

"Are you suggesting I'm litigious?"

"Erm…yes," Josh admitted.

Kris was about to argue to the contrary, but he had to concede that Josh was right. Since he'd quit, he'd been threatening to take the network to court for everything from harassment to defamation of character, and on all fronts, the evidence was stacked in his favour. For now, though, those were empty threats; so long as the producers released him from his contract, he wouldn't take action against them. However, it had been two weeks and they were still 'in talks', which was frustrating, as he needed to put it behind him, although it did give him time to sort out the mess he'd made of his personal life. That brought his thoughts full circle and to the other reason he was more than happy to accommodate Josh for the day.

"Soooo," Kris began tentatively, "I wanted to ask you a favour, and it's a bit of a biggie."

"OK?"

"How would you feel about another house guest for Christmas?"

"Who?"

Kris nodded at Casper, who was once again staring at the Christmas pudding toy.

Josh shrugged. "I don't see why not. We'll have to run it by George, of course, but Casper and Blue are best buddies, and I imagine after spending today with Sean's cat, Monty should be able to tolerate anything." Blue was George's dog, a young yet placid German shepherd. He was a gentle giant, in complete contrast to George's mum's little white Westie, Monty, who could be quite feisty but was generally all right once the initial growling receded, which was a fairly apt profile of George's mum too. "I take it you're all going away?" Josh asked.

"Yep. It's a surprise, though, so I can't say anything more just yet."

"A surprise for Shaunna or Ade?"

"Shaunna. Ade knows about it."

"Oh? I'm intrigued." Josh watched Kris carefully as he made their drinks, trying to glean more information.

Kris laughed and shook his head. "Pack it in!"

Josh grinned. They took their drinks over to the table, and Josh moved his laptop and papers to free up some space.

"Have you managed to get much done?" Kris nodded at Josh's work.

"Yes. I'm more or less finished. Just giving it a final check before I email it to the editor." Josh squinted at the topmost page of print and sighed. "Damn it." He popped the lid off a highlighter and ran it across a line of text. "Every time I look at the thing, I find something else."

Kris leaned in to read the highlighted section. It looked OK to him. "What's it about?"

"Friendship as a determinant of social readjustment and resilience."

Kris nodded slowly. "Right." He had no clue what that meant.

"In other words, how friends get you through the bad times."

"Ah, now if you'd said that in the first place…" Kris joked self-consciously. Without his friends, he simply wouldn't have made it this far in his life. Indeed, there was one very special friend who deserved not just an apology but to know the truth, even though the prospect of delivering it made Kris feel physically sick.

Although Josh's attention appeared to be on his research, Kris could tell he was under scrutiny and was glad he had a reason to leave. "I'm gonna have this and get out of your way," he said, raising his voice to compensate for the squeaking of the Christmas pudding toy. Casper had finally figured it out, and now there was no stopping him. "I'm meeting Ade in town," Kris shouted over the din.

Josh nodded to show he had heard.

After that, they sat and drank in silence, which was to say they didn't bother trying to converse any further; Casper was making far too much noise for that to be possible. Kris finished his tea and gave Josh an apologetic smile.

"See you later," he said, making a quick getaway from the squeaking.

"Bye." Josh watched Casper throw the Christmas pudding up in the air and squash it with his paw as it hit the floor. He had a feeling his day of quiet working had just come to a premature end.

***

Hayley put down the phone and swore under her breath. Shaunna heard her, but she was with a customer and carried on listening to the woman's monologue about grandchildren's Christmas lists and online videos from Santa, humming and smiling back at her in the mirror as appropriate. Anyone watching would have thought she was paying no attention whatsoever, but she was taking it all in, genuinely amazed at how much things had changed since Krissi was little.

"There you go, hun," she said, removing the protective cape from the woman's shoulders. "All done."

"And stunning, as usual," the woman complimented.

Shaunna smiled bashfully. She swapped the cape for her customer's very heavy and expensive coat. "Now, you have a lovely Christmas." She held the coat whilst the woman slipped her arms into the sleeves.

"And you, Shaunna." The woman opened her bag and took out a bottle-shaped gift. "This is a little thank-you for your perseverance in trying to keep me looking young and beautiful."

"Oh!" Shaunna took the gift from her and blushed. "You really shouldn't have, but thank you!"

"I recall you mentioning your favourite tipple. I hope this will suffice."

"Can I open it now?"

The woman nodded her consent, and Shaunna peeled back the paper, revealing a bottle of what looked like—and probably was—expensive vintage red wine.

"It was in the wine cellar," the woman explained, "and I thought you'd enjoy it more than me, so there you are." She looked pleased with herself.

"Well that's very kind of you." Shaunna and the customer exchanged a continental kiss near each cheek, booked a next appointment for New Year's Eve, and the woman toddled off up the road to her husband's waiting BMW.

Shaunna examined the vintage wine in her hand and shook her head at the pointless expense of it, big cars, and everything else that today seemed so frivolous. Last night, when she'd been out doing the last of her Christmas shopping, she'd come across a homeless girl with a stray kitten. The pair of them had been soaked to the skin, and the kitten looked sick, yet Shaunna had been reluctant to give the girl money, convinced it wouldn't help her in the longer term, given she smelled strongly of alcohol even though she couldn't have been more than fifteen.

It was only after the girl had gone that it dawned on Shaunna. She could have helped in some other way—bought her a meal or offered to pay for a taxi so she could get to a hostel—and she'd kept an eye out on the way down to the milk bar, but the girl had disappeared into the cold night air. It hadn't stopped Shaunna from thinking about her, though, and as soon as she got to Andy's, she went online and sent a donation to The Children's Society, not knowing what else to do and feeling utterly hopeless.

"That was the manicurist, sweedie." Hayley's voice brought Shaunna back from her thoughts. "She can't make it due to the snow."

"Damn." That was going to be a major problem. "I suppose I could do the nails," Shaunna suggested.

Hayley shook her head, her heavily lacquered bob moving as one. "I need you on hair, sweedie."

"Have you tried Carla?"

"Yah. Booked solid. What about that beaudician pal of yours?"

"Adele?" Shaunna was pretty sure the answer would be no. Adele didn't need the money and would likely be enjoying her day off watching Christmas movies with her three-year-old daughter—Shaunna's namesake—but she didn't know anyone else who could do acrylic nails to a professional standard, and they were desperate. She took her phone out of her pocket and brought up Adele's number. "Hiya, hun. You OK?"

"Yes, thanks. You?"

"I'm fine. Listen, are you free this afternoon for a couple of hours?"

"I can be. Why?"

"We've got a hen party coming in at two, and the manicurist has let us down. I'm really sorry to ask, but—"

"Of course!" Adele interrupted.

"Oh!" Shaunna was far too amazed to disguise it.

"I'll have to bring Shu with me if that's all right? Dan's working."

"Yeah, that's fine," Shaunna confirmed, and it would be—so long as Shu's Uncle Andy didn't end up taking off too many clothes. Shaunna felt herself getting all flustered at the thought of it. "She'll be in her element. Thanks, hun. I love you lots."

"Love you too. See you soon." Adele hung up.

"Sorted," Shaunna said.

Hayley sighed in relief. "Fab, sweedie." She gave Shaunna a hug—at least the fifth of the day. "I suppose we should ged ourselves a liddle lunch while we can."

7. Candy-Caned

ANDY CAREFULLY SLOWED the Mustang to a stop outside Milky's. The council had re-gritted the town centre but appeared to have run out before they reached the end of the high street, and driving conditions were perilous.

Kris, in the passenger seat, peered past Andy and spotted Ade through the vast plate-glass window fronting the milk bar. The neon *Milky*'s sign glowed warm and bright in the chilly dark of the midwinter afternoon, deep-pink light flaring across Kris's line of sight so that Ade seemed to sparkle as he emerged in a haze of escaped heat, putting on his coat whilst he gracefully traversed the pavement, at speed and without slipping. He opened the back door of the Mustang and climbed in behind Andy.

"Well, this definitely surpasses trudging through six inches of snow." Ade glanced around him appreciatively and smoothed his hand over the black leather seat.

Kris and Andy gave each other a knowing look.

"Front and rear seat belts," Ade observed, fastening one around him. "This is a '69, isn't it?"

"Yeah," Andy confirmed. "I had the rear belts fitted in case I ever have kids in the back." He realised the implication of what he'd said and elaborated, "You know…my niece…or whoever."

"And authentic Mustang belts too," Ade noted, completely missing Andy's uncharacteristic floundering. They didn't know each other that well, which would no doubt change in time, what with Kris and Shaunna's continued closeness and Andy and Ade's shared enthusiasm for classic cars. Since Ade had retired his MG, he'd had a couple of small, modern hatchbacks but neither suited, and he was currently 'between cars'. At some point, he'd make a concerted effort to find one he liked, but for the most part, he could manage without a car on a practical level, and those he did like were more recreational.

"You can't beat the classics," he mused aloud.

"No, you can't," Andy agreed.

"My dream car is the E-Type Jaguar."

"Yeah?" Andy glanced at Ade in the rear-view mirror, but he was otherwise occupied with admiring the Mustang and continued to do so all the way back to the house—a journey that took much longer than usual. Contrary to Shaunna's worries about Andy's speed-limit excesses, he was taking things very slowly.

"Do you want me to come and pick you up later?" Andy offered once they'd stopped.

Kris peered behind him at Ade. "What d'you think?"

"We'll be OK walking, won't we?" Ade said.

"I suppose so." Kris was less than pleased with the prospect of trudging through ice and snow in below-zero temperatures.

"I'm sure you have a pair of fabulous, super-grippy Scandinavian boots somewhere, babe."

"Ooh! Actually, I do. Good thinking." Kris turned back to Andy. "We'll walk up and meet you after the salon closes. About six at the pub?"

"Cool. Send me a text if you change your mind."

"Will do. And thanks."

"No worries."

Kris gave Andy a meaningful smile. Ade saw it but waited until they were out of the car and Andy had pulled away before he said anything.

"What was that about?"

"What?" Kris asked, feigning ignorance.

Ade already had his key in his hand and unlocked the door, stepping aside so Kris could tackle Casper. "You and Andy?"

Kris peered along the hallway to the empty kitchen, where he'd expected to find Josh still toiling away. "Nothing," he said cagily.

Ade took the hint and let it be, for now. "We're home alone?" he asked instead.

"Apparently so."

It looked like Josh had left a while ago, as the kettle was cold, and the man drank enough coffee to singlehandedly keep a café in business.

Even though it was empty, the house was still warm and cosy, with a faint scent of vanilla and cinnamon drifting from the unlit candles in the living room. Ade took out his lighter—he rarely smoked these days but still kept it for occasions like this—and lit the candles.

Kris switched on the tree lights and headed for the door, his intention to go and make drinks, but Ade hooked him by the shirt collar on the way past and pulled him back. Rather than ask outright, he gave Kris an enquiring look.

Kris put his arms around him and kissed him on the nose. "I was going to get the kettle on."

"Was it about what happened the other day?"

"Y-yeah, it was," Kris stuttered. He'd only told Ade about his second visit to Andy, and whilst coming clean was on his 'un-screwing-up agenda', he wasn't ready yet. He opted for a change of subject, which wasn't any better, but he wanted to warn Ade in advance. "I'm going to tell George about Anders."

Ade leaned back to look Kris in the eye. "Why?"

"He deserves to know."

"But what purpose is served by telling him?" Kris nuzzled into Ade's shoulder, and Ade nudged him. "Will it make you feel better?" Kris shrugged. "OK. When are you going to tell him?"

"Nm-nm-ner," Kris mumbled incoherently.

Ade chuckled. "When was that?"

Kris lifted his head and repeated, "Tomorrow."

"Do you want me to come with you?"

"You're meeting Pip."

"I can postpone if you need me."

"No, it's fine, but thank you. Shaunna and Josh will be there. We'll be OK...I hope." Kris was trying to convince himself, as he could feel the panic rising at the thought of it, but he was at the point where only drastic measures would do. All his life, he'd believed that a career breakthrough would bring with it the healing he so desperately yearned—proof he was worth something in his own right—more than a friend, a husband, a substitute father—but it hadn't. It had merely served as a poultice, drawing everything to the surface, and now the whole world had seen what an almighty fuck-up Kristian Johansson was. It was only through the love and perseverance of the people he cared most about that he'd been able to cling to a barely tangible hope he wasn't a total waste of air and space.

Kris knew what he was doing was selfish. He needed George to understand there was a reason behind his shameful behaviour. Through everything Kris had done—the good and the bad—George had stood by him. He'd kept secrets for him, defended and forgiven him, and Kris hoped by explaining, he might vindicate George's enduring faith in him. More than that, he wanted George to know how important his friendship was.

"Will you?" Ade asked, seemingly apropos of nothing, but he'd been watching Kris and waiting for the thought process to play out.

"Will I?" Kris repeated with a frown.

"Be OK telling George."

"Oh!" Kris smiled and nodded. "Yeah. Thank you. So what are your and Pip's plans? Shop till you drop?"

"Yes, that, and lunch, and too many sweeties, and gingerbread lattes..."

Ade's face lit up with a bright, happy smile as he slipped into reminiscing Christmas Eves past, for several years now spent with Pip, the best friend who had dragged him through the horror of his previous relationship. Truthfully, without her, Ade wouldn't have made it, which was why he could understand Kris's reliance on his friends, and none more so than George. They were each other's first boyfriend, and that intimacy had tattooed itself onto their friendship, but Ade trusted them both completely. Even if George were available—and one only had to catch a passing glimpse of George and Josh together to know how very unavailable he was—Kris could barely cope with one relationship, never mind an affair or the 'sharing' arrangement they'd attempted during the past few months. Just thinking about it made Ade squirm a little with embarrassment, although dire situations called for dire solutions, and it had seemed a good idea at the time.

Thankfully, it was all done with now. In the two weeks since Kris had finished working on *Shadows*, his behaviour and thinking had been erratic and often frighteningly irrational, but it was all part of him fighting back. He was trying—perhaps not always in the best or most sensible way—to make things right, and telling George about the abuse was evidently a part of that process. It didn't make for an especially merry Christmas, though, and Ade was relieved Kris hadn't asked him to cancel his plans with Pip, not that they extended beyond anything more than their usual shop and eat, and shop, and eat, until they were ready to explode, or collapse—it could go either way.

As Ade emerged from his thoughts, he remembered where the conversation had started, and how deftly Kris had changed the subject. "I'm still intrigued by your little secret with Andy."

"Who says we have a secret?"

"You do. Or your face does, at least. You didn't come on to him again, did you?"

"Hey! I didn't come on to him a first time, if you don't mind!"

Ade laughed at Kris's indignation. He was teasing. "So...?" He tickled Kris until he bucked away. "Ve haff vays..."

Kris hugged his arms to his sides, squeaking and giggling. "Ade! Stop!" he pleaded. He was very ticklish, and both Shaunna and Ade used it against him.

"Not till you tell me."

"You know how it's nearly Christmas?"

"Hmm?"

"And you know how people buy each other presents?"

"Hmm?"

"That's all," Kris finished. He was laughing so much it hurt, but he wasn't going to relent.

Ade realised it was pointless and gave up. "You didn't tell him about their present either?" he asked.

"Nope. I just told him to make sure he had the necessary documentation." Kris chewed his lip, worrying. "I hope they like it."

Ade stilled the chewing with his own lips. "They'll love it, babe, I'm certain. So...three hours of the house to ourselves..." He stepped back and took Kris's hands, surprised by how cold they were. "They're like ice!"

"Baby, it's cold outside," Kris responded tunefully with a grin, his eyes sparkling in the candlelight. Ade laughed.

"Well, I am most definitely staying. What would you like to do?"

And just like that, Kris's prior jovial mood evaporated.

"Babe?" Ade had no idea what he'd said to provoke such a reaction.

"Do you promise?" Kris asked.

Ade shook his head. "Promise what?"

"That you'll stay." Kris looked petrified.

"I'm not going anywhere," Ade assured him.

Kris smiled and attempted to rally. "How about a Christmas movie? Hot chocolate, popcorn..."

Ade nodded in agreement and placed a gentle kiss on Kris's cheek. "Sounds perfect."

***

Shu—or 'Little Shaunna', as she was formally known—was truly in her element. Hayley had given her one of the practice plastic heads the apprentices used, and Shu was standing on a chair at the end of the line of mirrors, next to grown-up Shaunna, endeavouring to replicate the motion of the curling tongs with a set of her own—not plugged in.

"What a beautiful job you've done," the bride's mother praised. Shu grinned and went at it with a little more vigour.

Meanwhile, the bride and chief bridesmaid were telling Adele all about 'The Wedding Dress Fiasco', while Adele worked on the bride's nails and passed comment on the attitude of the dress shop being 'simply unacceptable'. She would never tell a bride that the only way she was going to get down from a size fourteen to a twelve in two weeks was liposuction.

Of course, had Adele met the bride two weeks rather than twenty-four hours before the wedding, she could have shared some tips on cutting out carbs and detoxing that would have done the trick. As it was, the best advice she could offer was to purchase a corset from the department store, and to mention Adele's name to the manager of Lingerie, as it would probably get her a discount. The bride was delighted, although truth be told, Adele thought it unlikely a size twelve would go near her this side of New Year.

Kelly, the beautician, was set up in the back-left corner of the salon with a couple of black vinyl recliners, where two of the bride's friends were presently relaxing with a glass of champagne each. Christmas music was playing, everyone was chatting, and there was a great party feeling, enhanced by the snowy exterior that glistened all the more for the condensation clouding the front windows.

Adele gave the bride's nails a final coating of shellac and shared a glass of champagne with her whilst they waited for Shaunna and Hayley to finish with the bride's mother and sister. Then it was all change.

Shaunna took the bride over to wash her hair, noticing that she looked a little upset. "Are you OK?" she asked quietly, easing the woman back against the sink and subtly watching her while testing the warmth of the water against her palm.

"Yes," came the gasped response, but the question had set off the tears.

Shaunna switched off the water. "I'll just show you where the loo is," she said cheerily, for the benefit of anyone who might be listening, and led the bride out back, away from everyone else. Shaunna said nothing further but remained close by as the poor woman sobbed into a tissue, chastising herself for being silly.

"I'm sorry," she said. "I really am happy about the wedding. But it's so stressful!"

"Yeah, it is," Shaunna agreed.

"Are you married?"

"I am. We're separated, but still good friends."

"Did you feel like this?"

"A little bit. My friend Adele—the one who's just done your nails—she got married a few years ago, and she was a complete mess right up until the day of the wedding."

"Is she still with him?"

"Err, no." Shaunna mentally kicked herself. "But whatever," she added quickly, "it's hard work getting married, both physically and mentally. Most brides feel exactly the same as you do."

"Honestly?"

"Yep. And I've met a few, working here."

The woman nodded and attempted a smile. "I was so scared I was making a mistake, but I guess it's only pre-wedding jitters."

"I imagine so. You just have to ask yourself, do I want to spend the rest of my life with this person? If the answer is yes, then you're doing the right..." She trailed off at the sound of a shrill squeal that came from the shop.

"What on earth was that?" the bride asked.

Shaunna grinned. "The entertainment's arrived. Are you ready, or do you want me to leave you a bit longer?"

"No, I'm OK now, thanks. You know, you should seriously think about becoming a counsellor. You're very good at it."

"Thanks!" Shaunna led the way back through to everyone else. "I'm actually studying a psychology course, although I love working here."

"Whatever makes you happy."

They both stopped in the doorway between the stockroom and the salon, watching Andy flip Shu the right way up and return her to the floor.

"Go on, trouble." Andy waited for her to toddle back to her 'client' and then lifted his eyes to meet Shaunna's. "I hear you've been having a problem with one of the dryers," he said, a smile teasing his lips.

"Yeah," Shaunna confirmed breathlessly. The bride was still standing next to her and grabbed her arm.

Andy took off his hard hat and shook his hair loose. "I guess I won't be needing that." He placed the hat on a shelf and slowly unzipped his jacket.

"Oh. My. God!" the bride whispered loudly into Shaunna's ear. They both started giggling.

"Erm…" Adele said loudly, "Shaunna?"

"Yeah?" Shaunna answered without taking her eyes off the sexy vision before her.

"Do I need to blindfold my daughter?"

"No, hun."

"OK. Just thought I'd check."

Andy turned and gave Adele a cheeky wink. She started giggling too and blushed bright pink.

"It's that dryer," Shaunna said, pointing to her right somewhere. Andy nodded and whipped off his jacket, revealing a pair of heavy cargo pants, currently held up by braces, and a tight, white vest. Shaunna swallowed and tried to breathe slowly.

"That one?" Andy repeated.

Shaunna nodded, completely cut off from the activity going on around her, which consisted of eight women swooning, Shu singing to her 'client' and Hayley looking utterly delighted by the reception Andy was receiving. He moved away towards the dryers, all eyes on him, and Shaunna, incredibly, managed to snap herself out of it.

"Shall we, err, go wash your hair?" she suggested to the bride.

"If we must," the bride replied with a grin. "But make it quick. I don't want to miss a thing!"

Shaunna laughed and steered the woman back to the sink, washed her hair in record time and got her sat down so she could watch Andy's reflection in the mirror.

By this point, he had the hood off the dryer, and one of his braces was hanging loose at his side, the other still on his shoulder, but that wouldn't last. He paused to wipe the sweat from his brow, his vest riding up at the front and revealing a little of his taut lower abs and the treasure trail of dark hair running from his belly button. Shaunna followed it down, eyeing the bulge hungrily, and remembered to breathe. Hayley trotted over and handed Andy a cold can of drink.

"Cheers," he said, popping the ring-pull and glugging thirstily. There were groans from all directions. Andy adjusted his pants, pulling them up and forward so they were tighter across his buttocks and lower at the front.

The bride's mother looked set to pass out. Adele watched Shaunna in the mirror until she got her attention and gave her a grin.

Shaunna shook her head, laughing to herself, and continued with the bride's restyle. Her own hair, usually securely tied back, had partly escaped its clip and was hanging in wisps around her face, but she'd noticed Andy looking her over and decided to leave it for his benefit. The next time she properly paid attention to him, the other brace was off, the waistband of his boxers was visible above his low-slung cargo pants, and he had worked up enough of a sweat to be gleaming under the lights.

The champagne was flowing, the women were all having a fabulous time, and Andy was enjoying himself, as was Hayley. She'd already had one of the bride's friends ask about booking a fortieth birthday party, on the proviso that the 'entertainment' came as part of the package. That last word had made Hayley glance across to see what the 'package' was, and she was having something of a problem keeping her eyes off him.

It ceased to be a problem the minute the salon door swung open and Dan walked in. He drew to a halt, taking in the scene before him, whilst the women, who were very tipsy, looked from one to the other of the brothers in lusty-eyed wonder.

"Daddy!" Shu shouted and went running over to him. He swept her up and kissed her hot, rosy cheek.

"Hiya, baby girl," he said, then frowned at Andy. "Bro?"

"Yeah." Andy tried not to blush as he sidled over. "We're, err, branching out," he said quietly.

"I'm gonna assume this has nothing to do with fixing hairdryers?"

Andy gave him a wry smile. "Gotta get back to it," he said and returned to his 'work'.

Dan put his daughter down, and she went to her mum, who had been painting little glittery stars on her nails for her.

"You OK for a bit?" Dan asked Adele. She nodded to indicate she was. Dan nodded back. "I'd best give you a hand," he said to his brother, removing his jacket and flinging it at Hayley.

The bride and her fellow hens whooped and wolf-whistled. Hayley was grinning from ear to ear. Dan was wearing his usual casual shirt over a tight muscle tee, and he was broader than Andy, with more definition, so when he took off his shirt, the noise level went through the roof. Dan and Andy looked at each other, both feeling a little self-conscious but revelling in the attention and the compliments they were getting.

"You know, if we were women, this would be completely out of order," Dan said under his breath.

"Yeah," Andy agreed. "Just as well we're not, hey, bro?" He handed Dan the hood of the dryer, which was the last part to put back in place.

Dan hoisted it up on his shoulder and posed, with biceps flexed, as he watched his brother work. "Wanna take it up a notch?" he asked.

Andy raised an eyebrow. "Go for it."

Dan passed the hood back to Andy, got down on the floor and slid on his back between Andy's legs.

"I'll hold it steady," he said, pushing up on the underside of the dryer, the outline of his six-pack enhanced by the tight, black T-shirt.

Andy leaned forward and tightened the bolt with a ratcheted socket, deliberately thrusting forward with each twist. He glanced down at his brother's grinning face.

"Damn, that's hot!" the chief bridesmaid said loudly and then covered her mouth. The other women laughed.

"How's your ego holding out down there?" Andy asked.

"About the same size as yours now, I reckon." Dan winked. "Give me a hand up."

Andy reached down and took Dan's opposite hand, pulling him to his feet. They gave each other a manly clap on the back, officially marking the end of the show. The women all applauded, and Shaunna brought the bride over to meet them.

"Thank you so much," she said, no trace of her earlier tears. They each gave her a hug and a kiss on the cheek. "Great with kids, practical and sexy to boot. You two are just about as perfect as they come!"

8. Not Even a Peep

WHILE HAYLEY, SHAUNNA, Adele and Kelly tidied away, the six members of the hen party thanked Andy and Dan for the show, some—including the bride's mother—drunk enough to risk a quick squeeze of biceps or bottom pinch on their way out. After they'd gone, Hayley gave both brothers a heartfelt hug.

"You were udderly wonderful," she gushed, dividing the cash payment and tips into several piles. She handed one to Kelly the beautician.

"Thanks, Hayley." Kelly gave Hayley and Shaunna a hug and kiss. "Merry Christmas."

"And to you, hun," Shaunna replied.

Andy went out and helped Kelly de-ice her car; she had a little old Fiesta with lousy heating, and it was bitterly cold. He returned, shivering and rubbing his bare arms to warm them, only stopping when Hayley beckoned to him with a wad of notes. He looked at it and frowned. "That's way too much."

"No, sweedie. You just quadrupled our tips. Go buy this lovely gal of yours something extra-special."

"Fair enough." He took the money and handed half of it to Dan. "Stick that in Shu's trust fund for me?"

Dan stuffed the money in his back pocket. "It's been fun," he said.

"So you'd be up for doing it again?" Hayley hedged.

Andy looked at Dan, and they both shrugged. "Sure. Why not?"

Hayley clapped her hands together in delight.

"Right. We'd best make tracks." Dan lifted his daughter with one arm and Adele's acrylic nails cases with the other.

"OK, bro. See you tomorrow," Andy said.

Dan gave him a quick nod, and followed Adele out to the car, pausing so Shu could wave at her Uncle Andy.

"Now, sweedie," Hayley addressed Shaunna, "are you sure you're OK closing up?"

"No problem, Hayles. You go and have fun."

"Thanks. I'll tell you all about it in the morning."

Hayley gathered her belongings and she, too, was on her way. Shaunna picked up the floor brush and started from the door.

"What else needs doing?" Andy asked.

"Not much. Just this, and the sinks need a quick clean."

He took the brush from her. "You go do the sinks. I'll brush up."

She kissed his cheek. "Thanks."

"No worries."

He worked his way to the back of the shop, arriving at the stockroom door at the same time she did with the dustpan and brush. With much touching and kissing and teasing, they eventually scooped up the small pile of debris and went into the stockroom to put the brushes away. The stockroom door swung to a close, and Shaunna put her arms around Andy's neck.

"My goodness," she breathed. Her lips touched his as she spoke. "You are some seriously hot eye candy!"

He smiled and kissed her at the same time. "You liked that, huh?"

"Liked it?" She allowed him to steer her back against the shelving. "If I was a man, I'd have been keeping that hard hat in front of me."

Andy reached up and removed her hairclip, letting her soft curls tumble over his bare arm. He pushed against her and kissed her hard.

"You could do with the hard hat yourself," she said in between the kisses.

"I've got nothing to hide." He unzipped her tunic, and she wriggled her shoulders free. The fabric slipped away, revealing her bra. Andy paused to admire the sight before him, running his hands over the soft red velvet barely covering her breasts and tracing the white frilly outline of the cups with his fingertips.

"Festive," he murmured as he casually unhooked the straps. Her bra started to slide with the push-pull of their bodies grinding against each other.

"It's a matching set," she explained, lifting on her arms so he could take off her work pants.

"So it is." He released them, along with the skimpy red knickers, and returned his attention to her cleavage, alternating between kissing and running his tongue down between her breasts.

She squeezed them together and trapped him. "The front door's still unlocked."

"Who's gonna come in now? It's gone half five."

"They might still try the door."

"Let them," he said. He unfastened his cargos and hooked her bare legs around him.

She glanced down at his erection, and up again at his lust-glazed expression. "You like the idea of getting caught?"

He shrugged. "Maybe."

In spite of her protest, she offered no resistance and was so aroused that he slid straight into her. She let out a loud moan, pushing up onto him, keeping her hands jarred against the shelves to gain some thrust. Her nipples peeked above the lace-edged bra cups, and she arched her back, causing them to brush against the fabric of his vest.

"You really did enjoy watching me," Andy said, although it was more of a grunt. It was a serious turn-on.

"Oh, God, yes," she panted, lifting herself higher.

He put his arms behind her and increased his speed, every bang of his hips met by a gasp of pleasure, each one increasing in volume the faster they moved together. Her hands roamed under his vest, which clung to him with the sweat of working in the salon and the physical exertion of trying to simultaneously give her as much as he could and hold back.

Each time he tried to back away, she grabbed him and pulled him in again. Her breasts bounced freely against his chest. The shelves squeaked under duress, accompanied by the slap together of buttocks and thighs and her cries of pleasure, until he had no choice but to enter the final rapid build to climax, now too far gone to worry about anyone disturbing them or hearing her shouting.

***

Kris and Ade stopped outside the salon. They were a little early arriving for their prearranged evening of reconciliation and drinks, so they'd decided to walk down and meet Shaunna and Andy, and it was cold. Kris pushed the door to see if it was open; it was. He shrugged and stepped inside. Ade followed, the sound of the traffic slowly fading out as the door closed behind them. Kris took in a breath, preparing to call through to the stockroom to announce their arrival, but the sounds he heard coming from that direction instantly muted him. He closed his mouth and turned to Ade without a word.

"We should wait outside," Ade whispered.

Kris shook his head. "Not yet." He continued to listen to the yells of passion coming from the stockroom, aware of Ade staring at him, trying to make sense of his uncharacteristic voyeurism. The grunting and groaning increased in speed and intensity then fell away to rapid breathing, then silence. Ade walked out.

"Ade! Wait!" Kris tried to run after him, but the snow was re-freezing and it was too slippery. When he finally caught up, he grabbed Ade by the arm, but Ade shook him off. "Please. Let me explain."

Ade stopped but refused to face him. He was angry and hurt. For more than a year, he'd fought his jealousy of Kris and Shaunna and their mutual friends. Kris had ended it once, out of fear of losing them, and Ade could deal with that. He *had* dealt with it, and with the three of them living together. He'd given it his best shot because he loved Kris, and he cared a lot for Shaunna, but he'd laid it on the line when he came back: if he had to walk away again, that would be it. This situation was enough to make him walk.

"Please?" Kris pleaded.

Ade turned back. "Why?" he asked, still refusing to look at Kris. "What the hell do you get from listening to them fucking? Is it some kind of torture? Are you punishing yourself? Or do you get off on it?"

"What? No! It's none of those things." Kris tried to take Ade's hand again, but he jerked away. "Please, Ade. It's…" Kris put his head down. "All the time I was with her, I could hear it. Her protests against him. Making love to her was so bloody tough. I tried to be gentle, always so careful to make sure it was her choice, that I wasn't forcing her into doing something she didn't want to. That's what I meant about the difference—am I being too much of a man or not enough? But I got it all wrong. All so fucking wrong. Should I have been rougher with her? Is that what she wanted all along?"

Ade laughed, purely from disbelief. "What the hell has that got to do with perving on them having sex?"

"Did it sound like screams of pain and protest to you?"

"Of course it didn't!"

"That's what I mean."

Andy had just backed out of the salon door and was waiting for Shaunna to lock up. He noticed Kris and Ade and waved. They waved back.

"Look," Kris said quietly, "I don't know how else to explain it to you, but I promise I wasn't doing it because it turned me on. It's eating me up that I never understood before. I didn't give her what she needed, and I lost her because of it."

"And now you want her back?"

"No. I want her to be happy, and she is. With Andy."

"Yet you still regret fucking it up? How does that work?"

"I'm a mess, and I lost her because of it. And I'm going to get help because I can't lose you too." Kris turned away to hide that he was about to break down. "I don't want to lose you, Ade. I love you."

***

Shaunna and Andy stayed where they were, watching Kris and Ade. It looked like they were fighting.

"I'm still not sure about this going out for a drink together," Shaunna said quietly.

"Let's just stay for one," Andy suggested. "Sort out times for tomorrow."

"Tomorrow?"

"I'm giving them a lift to Manchester."

"Are you?"

"Yeah. Will you come with me?"

"What for?"

"Because I'm your boyfriend?"

Shaunna gave him a weary look, and he grinned.

"And because I'd like your company."

She sighed. "I s'pose I'll have to." Kris and Ade were on their way back to them. "This is gonna be fun..." she muttered.

"So, I thought we could maybe head back your way, Andy?" Kris suggested lightly, trying to gloss over what he knew they had witnessed, and to hide his shame at his own behaviour. "That way, you can leave your car at home and have a drink with us."

"Sounds good," Andy said.

They all piled into the Mustang, which was wonderful and showy, but it still hadn't warmed up by the time they arrived at the apartments and piled out again.

Shaunna looped her arm through Ade's. "'Sup?" she asked.

He shook his head. "I'll tell you later," he mumbled, and she let it go.

The pub was only a short walk up the road, and when they reached it, Andy fought his way through the crowd to buy the first round. He decided he'd risk a beer, seeing as he wasn't driving and he didn't have to think so hard about his behaviour around Shaunna anymore, although she'd opted for orange juice and lemonade. They were both feeling uneasy about being 'together' in Kris's presence.

With two glasses in each hand, Andy edged away from the bar and scanned the pub for the others. Kris waved to attract his attention. They'd got lucky and secured a table in the far corner, where the four of them quickly settled into chatting about nothing of great importance. It was an effort doing that much, with the awkwardness of all that had gone before.

Ade was noticeably subdued and jumped on the chance to buy the next round. Shaunna went to the bar with him, leaving Andy and Kris alone.

For a few minutes, Andy and Kris watched the people around them. The pub was packed with revellers: a few groups out on work Christmas nights, all very merry and in full festive attire; women in glittery tops and men donning Christmas ties. There was a good atmosphere, and it went some way towards easing the discomfort they were feeling. Kris caught Andy's gaze and attempted a smile.

"You alright, mate?" Andy asked.

Kris nodded, although it was clear he wasn't.

Andy looked over at Ade and Shaunna, both giggling at a woman who was doing things to her boss that she was probably going to regret tomorrow. Shaunna leaned in and whispered something to Ade; he gasped dramatically and slapped her arm.

"You go for the same type," Andy observed.

"What d'you mean?"

"Shaunna and Ade. They're a lot like each other. Outgoing, down to earth, clever, flirty…"

"Sex mad," Kris finished. Andy raised an eyebrow. "I heard you. In the salon?"

"Ah." Andy turned a strange colour—the consequence of blushing and going pale at the same time.

"I thought I should own up because I didn't just hear you. I stayed and listened."

Andy folded his arms defensively. "Why?"

"You didn't rape her."

"Sorry?"

"At the party. What I heard then was no different to what I heard tonight."

"Hang on a minute. She was drunk. I had no right—"

"And so were you, allegedly."

"No allegedly about it, mate. I was out of my skull. It doesn't excuse what I did."

"No, but my point is she made a hell of a lot of noise, and I thought she was trying to fight you off. It turns out she's just really noisy when she's screwing you."

Now Andy blushed for real. Kris laughed, ashamed but glad he'd confessed.

Andy's embarrassment started to subside, and he leaned forward to speak. "She is a bit loud, isn't she?"

"With you! Never with me."

"Really?" Andy rubbed his chin, trying not to show how proud that made him feel, but Kris caught it anyway.

"And yeah, you're right. They are a lot alike," he said with a wink.

Andy grinned. "He's a screamer?"

"That's one way of putting it."

At that, they both started laughing, although Shaunna and Ade were on their way back, so they had to contain it to some extent. Nevertheless, it had broken the ice.

Shaunna sensed things were a little better between the four of them, and as she sat, she lifted Andy's arm so that it was around her shoulders, glancing subtly at Kris to see how he reacted. He gave her the slightest of nods and picked up his drink, reaching for Ade's hand at the same time. Ade was still very cool with him but allowed it.

"If you ever start talking to me again," Kris said, "I want to ask you something."

Ade sighed loudly for effect. "I'll get over it. But you'd better have bought me something amazing for Christmas."

Kris smiled and kissed him on the cheek. "I love you," he whispered. "I really, really do." Ade tutted. "Lots and lots, like jelly tots." Kris started kissing his cheek over and over again, interspersed with repeats of "I love you."

Ade rolled his eyes and wiped his cheek dry. "OK! Stop. I forgive you."

"For what?" Shaunna asked.

Kris cleared his throat. "I did something stupid."

"Again?"

"Thanks!"

"You're welcome." Shaunna grinned. "So, what's all this about going to Manchester for Christmas?"

"We're going to Manchester for Christmas."

"And leaving me with the dog."

"Nope. Casper's going to stay at a friend's house."

"Whose?"

"Blue's."

"Since when?"

"Since Josh said it was OK. We'll have to check with George tomorrow, but I don't—"

73

Shaunna put up her hand to stop him. "Why? I'll still be at home."

"No, you won't."

"What?"

"I said, 'No, you won't.'"

"Kristian Johansson. Come this way," Shaunna got up and grabbed Kris by the scruff, leading him outside. It was pointless. He wasn't going to crack.

Ade waited until Shaunna and Kris were out of sight, then turned to Andy and grinned.

"I know where you're going," he sang.

"And I know what Kris has bought you for Christmas," Andy retorted.

"We could trade?" Ade offered.

"Not a chance. They'll string us up."

"Yes, you're probably right."

"You'd better believe it."

9. Deep Red Sea

CHRISTMAS EVE MORNING at the salon was not a lot of fun. Shaunna hadn't slept well—normal for her in the run-up to Christmas but exacerbated by the events of the past few days. She was more excited than anxious, which was an improvement, she supposed, although she was shattered, and Hayley was hungover.

During the course of the debaucherous ball Hayley had attended the previous evening, she'd lost the bracelet Marvin had bought her for their twenty-fifth wedding anniversary, and every so often, the guilt would hit her, or she'd remember something else embarrassing she'd said or done, put her hand to her head with an "EauhMaGaddd!" followed by an explanation. It amused Shaunna and their Christmas Eve regulars no end, but also made her glad they were closing at twelve thirty.

A little after midday, Kris arrived, carrying an oddly shaped bag that he said contained Hayley's present, which in no way explained the bag's curious outline. Shaunna's gift for her boss was a delicate rose gold and simulated pearl pendant, courtesy of Vincent the jeweller, who had given her a generous discount because she was one of 'Cordelia's girls'. Since meeting at Josh and George's wedding, Vincent and the retired school teacher had become good friends.

"This is gorgeous," Hayley gushed, holding the pendant against herself. "You don't see many good simuladed pearls, and you know how I am about the real deal, sweedie." She turned around, so Shaunna could fasten the clasp, and inspected herself in the nearest mirror. "Beaudiful," she said, giving Shaunna a hug. "Now you have a fabulous Christmas, sweedie, and I'll see you when you ged back."

"From?" Shaunna asked. Kris coughed into his hand.

"Uh, uh, uh-huh!" Hayley wagged her finger. "You'll just have to wait and see, sweedie. Ba-bye now."

With that, she ushered Shaunna out of the salon and flipped the closed sign on the door. Shaunna narrowed her eyes at Kris, but he was busy fishing in the bag. A moment later, he pulled out a set of brown felt antlers on a headband and passed them to her, followed by a second pair that he kept for himself. He flicked the switch on the side and put them on his head, grinning at her and bobbing his head so that the flashing antlers bopped back and forth. Shaunna put on her pair, and the two of them set off for the bus stop.

"We look completely bonkers," she said, making a grab for Kris's arm as she slid on the ice. Kris laughed and kept hold of her.

"That's because we are completely bonkers."

"Speak for yourself!"

Kris's smile faded, and he was suddenly serious.

"Are you sure you're OK with doing this today?" she asked.

"Telling George?"

Shaunna nodded.

"Yeah. I want to get it over with. Are you?"

"Yep."

"OK. Then let's do this crazy thing."

They caught the next bus out to the village where Josh and George lived. It was a ten-minute journey, and neither of them spoke on the way. There was too much to think about and secrets to keep that could easily slip out, given the way they were both feeling.

The pavements in the village were even more treacherous than the ones in town, and they half walked, half ice-skated up the path to the front door. They both took in a breath and started singing 'We Wish You A Merry Christmas' at the exact same moment, and then burst into fits of giggles.

"I'm gonna miss the whole being in tune with each other thing," Shaunna said.

Kris took her hand and kissed it. "Me too, although 'in tune' might be pushing it a bit."

Shaunna grinned and knocked on the door. "After three."

"Three," Kris said, and they started singing again, opening the door at the same time. Kris waved their offering of an enormous bottle of sherry as he poked his antlers around the doorpost. Shaunna followed suit, and they both stepped inside, still singing, but then Shaunna stopped, her grin replaced with an expression of total surprise.

"Red Sea Lady!"

Kris frowned and looked from Shaunna to the young girl who had uttered those words.

"Hello." Shaunna smiled in response, too shocked to come up with anything else. Never in a million years would she have guessed that these would be the 'visitors' Josh had warned her about in his earlier text message. The girl ran over and gave Shaunna an enormous hug. Shaunna reciprocated and raised her eyebrows at Kris, whose face was contorting into all manner of curious expressions.

"By any chance is this the girl you were talking about?" he asked nasally.

"It certainly is!" Shaunna said, glancing past her to the ginger kitten on the sofa. "And look at you!"

When she'd bumped into them in the shopping mall, Shaunna had been so convinced the cat would die, she was crying in joy and relief that they were both alive and seemingly well. However, quite what they were doing at Josh and George's was another matter.

"How did you end up here?" she asked the girl.

"George," she answered. "What you said about looking after each other? I promised we would and…" She looked back at the little cat. "I left Jinja, but he wouldn't leave me. Then I tried to take him to the animal shelter, but it was closed. If George hadn't helped us, I couldn't have looked after Jinja." She smiled at George. "And he couldn't have looked after me." She turned back to Shaunna and blinked, her eyes glistening with tears. "George saved our lives."

George blushed. "I wouldn't go quite that far," he mumbled bashfully.

"It's true," the girl argued. "If we'd still been on the street now, we'd have died of hypothermia."

Having just been out in the freezing cold, Kris and Shaunna were inclined to agree.

"It's going to be minus ten tonight," Kris said. He wriggled his nose, trying to hold back the sneeze and knowing the cat was the cause. It was no use. He sneezed.

"Just as well we've got all this sherry to warm us up, then," Shaunna said, passing the enormous bottle to Josh, who let his arm drop with the weight for effect.

"Can I have a little glass, please?" the girl asked.

George shook his head. "You're not old enough to drink."

"Children are allowed to drink alcohol at home with their parents."

"And would you be allowed to at home?"

"No, but I wouldn't be allowed to talk to homosexuals, either."

Shaunna started laughing, highly amused by the girl's bluntness. Kris sneezed again.

"Are you sure you'll be OK with the cat?" Josh asked.

Kris waved an arm to dismiss Josh's concern, then sneezed again, and again. "I'll be fine." After all, he hadn't stopped breathing, which was a major improvement on his past experience with cats, although he was starting to get a little wheezy.

"I'll go and sit upstairs with Jinja," the girl suggested.

"No. It's OK," Kris assured her. "It'll settle down in a—" another sneeze "—minute." Now his eyes were streaming.

"If I can borrow a pencil, I'll just stay in the study and draw. I don't mind."

"Are you sure?" George asked. She nodded and picked up her cat. George relented. "Come on, then. Let's get you a pencil and some paper."

"It's OK. I only need a pencil. I have something I need to finish today."

Their conversation faded away as they both ascended the stairs. Shaunna shrugged at Josh, and he quietly closed the living room door so he could speak freely.

"She ran away from home three and a half weeks ago. That's pretty much all we know."

"How old is she?"

"Not sure. She says she's seventeen."

"Closer to fifteen, I'd say."

"That's what I thought. However, there are no missing children matching her description. We had the duty social worker out last night. He was going to place her with an emergency foster carer, but she looked ready to bolt and told him she wanted to stay with George. We're both cleared to work with children, so the social worker agreed she could stay here until after Christmas."

"And then?"

"They'll investigate, I imagine." Josh suddenly realised Shaunna and Kris were still standing and had yet to take off their coats. "Are you two going to sit down?" he asked.

Reluctantly, they shuffled across the room and sat on the sofa, side by side.

Josh eyed them carefully. "Ohh. This is about more than looking after Casper, isn't it?"

Shaunna's reluctant nod confirmed it.

"We need to wait for George," Kris said.

Half a minute later, George returned and sat on the floor in front of the fire. He looked from one to the other of his friends, whose matching serious expressions meant it had to be bad news.

Shaunna gave him a smile of reassurance and took Kris's hand. "We need to tell you something, George, but first, we want to ask you a favour."

"Um, OK?"

"We've already cleared it with Josh."

George looked to Josh to see if it was true, not that he doubted Shaunna.

"The more the merrier by this point," Josh said.

With a frown, George turned back to Shaunna.

"Would you mind looking after Casper for us for a few days?"

"Ah!" Now he understood. Theirs was going to be a very full little house this Christmas, which, he decided, was exactly how it should be. "Are you going away?"

"Yep."

"Cool. Anywhere nice?"

"I'm going to Manchester," Kris said and then lowered his voice to add, "So not that nice, really."

"I heard that!" George's mum shouted on her way upstairs to use the bathroom.

That had been Kris's intent, as George's mum was a Mancunian through and through, and they actually got on very well. Or, at least, he got on with Iris Morley as well as anyone did. She had a habit of telling people what she thought, no holds barred, but her heart was in the right place. He smiled sweetly at her and she glowered in response.

George focused on Shaunna again. "So where are *you* going?" he asked.

"I don't know yet."

"OK." He was confused and, as usual, was completely tongue-tied.

"There's more."

"Right?"

"We're getting divorced." Before George could ask why, she explained, "In case we want to remarry."

"Oh." He tried to come up with something to say, but the words weren't there. "So, err…" He stopped and took another breath. "Is it…what I mean is…ah crap." He ran his hand over his head and huffed in annoyance. Knowing he had a medical condition that caused his wordlessness didn't make it any less frustrating to deal with.

There was a sudden flurry of movement as the girl came tearing back down the stairs, into the room, and stopped directly in front of George. The others watched the bizarre interchange in absolute amazement. It looked like she was using some kind of sign language, and when she was done, she gave George a hug, said, "Merry Christmas, cowboy," and left again.

"What was that about?" Kris asked.

George shrugged. "I've no idea."

"I have," Josh said but didn't elaborate; Shaunna was trying to gain his attention. He made eye contact with her and picked up the unspoken message. "Shaunna, come and give me a hand with this sherry?" he suggested.

She nodded and followed him from the room, leaving George and Kris alone to talk.

"What's happening?" Josh asked quietly once they were in the kitchen and out of earshot.

"Can you have a good mental breakdown?"

"Erm, let's see…" Josh's stance subtly changed from casual and friendly to professional and aloof, his finger resting on his chin as he pondered. Shaunna raised an eyebrow. "What?" he asked.

"You've gone all psychologist on me."

Josh shrugged. "You're the one talking shop, although I haven't exactly had a chance to wind down yet, with…" Josh glanced upwards, in the direction of his study. "In answer to your question, mental breakdown is a layperson's term, but if you refer to it as an 'acute psychological episode', then yes, I suppose you could have a good one. Why?"

"I think Kris is having one."

"I see." Josh took four glasses from the cupboard. "Tell me more."

"Actually, would you mind if I put the kettle on? I'd rather have a cuppa."

"Be my guest." Josh stepped aside, and Shaunna filled the kettle with water, continuing with her explanation whilst she waited for it to boil.

"OK, well, I'm guessing you've figured out me and Andy are having an affair."

"Really?" Josh gasped in mock horror. "No way!" Shaunna shoved him, and he grinned. "Yes, I did have a feeling you were. Although it's not really an affair if you and Kris are separated."

"Ah…" Shaunna chewed her lip and grimaced. "See, with Kris being a bit…loopy…Ade and I had this idea to…kind of…"

Josh stared at her with mouth open, aghast and amused. "You've been sharing him?"

"We've been sharing the burden," Shaunna clarified. "With the media constantly on his case and Jess and everything else, it's been really tough, and he was making crazy decisions. He'd got it into his head that if we divorced, Krissi would no longer want anything to do with him, even though she was completely fine with us separating and she loves Ade to bits. But it always comes back to the same thing."

"Andy?"

"Yep. So, anyway, the other day, Kris threatened him, and Andy finished things between us."

"Oh." Josh was listening to Shaunna, but they were also both aware of the increase in volume of the voices coming from the lounge.

Shaunna sped up and continued, "To cut a long story short, Kris apologised and got Andy to come and talk to me. Then last night, the four of us went to the pub together, and it was…well, it was really good fun, actually." Shaunna couldn't help but smile, and Josh hugged her.

"That's awesome," he said sincerely. "Is Andy taking you away for Christmas?"

"Your guess is as good as mine. He's not saying, but we're dropping Kris and Ade in Manchester later, and then…" She shrugged.

"Interesting." Josh picked up the three glasses of sherry but waited for Shaunna to make her tea before they slowly walked back along the hallway. "So what's this all about?" he whispered, nodding towards the lounge.

"Great-Uncle Anders," Shaunna whispered back.

"Oh, no." Josh's stomach flipped. As Dan's therapist, he'd known for a long time what Kris's great-uncle had put the two boys through, and for as much as he and George had no secrets, this was one thing he'd decided was best left in the drawer marked 'didn't come up'. And because it really hadn't come up, it was impossible to know if Kris had mentioned it to George before now, but Josh assumed, from the way Shaunna was talking, that he hadn't.

That fact was confirmed a few minutes after they re-entered the now silent lounge, where Kris was staring into the not-so-mesmerising depths of the gas fire, and George was focusing all his attention on stroking the dog. Shaunna resumed her place next to Kris and put a glass of sherry in his hand. A tear rolled down his face and dripped from his chin. George blinked and sniffed.

"I just don't…" he said and let out a very shaky sigh. He glanced up at Josh, eyes filled with pain and confusion. Josh smiled gently, trying to offer him comfort without pushing him over the emotional edge. George tried again. "Why didn't you tell me?"

Kris was still staring into the fire with tears running down his cheeks. He shook his head. "I didn't know how to," he said quietly. "I'm sorry." He put his head down and covered his eyes with his hand, his shoulders jolting with each sob. "I'm so sorry."

George shuffled on his knees around the coffee table and put his arms around Kris, pulling him close and sending the glass of sherry everywhere. Shaunna grabbed it and set it down on the table.

"What did you think I was gonna do?" George asked. Both he and Kris were crying so hard that they'd also set off Shaunna and Josh.

"I don't know. Dump me, I guess, for being too high maintenance."

George laughed through his tears. Kris was 'high maintenance' all the way, maybe partly for that reason, but it generally went with the territory of being creative, and they both were.

"I'm going to make coffee," Josh said, glancing at the sherry that had become too celebratory a drink. "You want more tea?" he asked Shaunna.

"I haven't touched this one yet, but I'll come and give you a hand."

"Beer here," George called after them.

"And for me," Kris said croakily.

Josh and Shaunna left the room again. George moved to sit next to Kris on the sofa. "Why did you decide to tell me now?"

"Part of my recovery."

"From?"

"Life?"

George had kept hold of Kris's hand when he moved, and he gave it a gentle rub to try and keep him in the here and now. He might only have been married to a psychologist, but George could interpret well enough the flinching eye movements as Kris fought painful flashbacks.

"Is that why you're getting divorced?"

"Yes." Kris frowned. "No." He turned so he could see George's face. "I knew I was losing it, and I went to see Dan to apologise for not standing up for him when it was happening. We had a long talk. He made me realise I've never properly dealt with it, and it got me thinking about everything else—why I wouldn't let Shaunna go so she could be with Andy, why I was so scared I was going to lose Krissi and all of you if we got divorced."

George's eyebrows rose. "Shaunna and Andy?"

"Yeah."

"How long's that been going on?"

"A couple of months."

"And you knew about it?"

"I did, but…" Kris looked away. "Shaunna and I were still sleeping together."

"You were…" George had been about to repeat what he'd heard, but as always, the words flew right away from him, and with them the thoughts of all that he wanted to say about it.

Kris knew him and knew exactly what he'd be thinking, so he said it for him. "Yes, it was greedy, and no, it's not because I'm bi. It wasn't even my idea. I went along with it because I was frightened of losing everything. And I know some bisexual people have successful polyamorous relationships, but they're not for me. They can be very painful for all concerned. And before you ask, I'm still sure I'm bisexual."

George opened and closed his mouth, momentarily imitating a goldfish.

Kris gave a small laugh. "I love you, George. You are such a wonderful friend, and you've put up with so much from me. I don't know why you've stuck around, but I'm glad you have. The last couple of years have been really hard, and I forgot about everyone else. It's been tough for all of us, and I should've said thank you. If you and Josh hadn't stepped in when I did what I did, I'd have ended up in prison. And instead of thanking you, I took advantage. I'm so grateful to you for—well, I don't even know where to start, to be honest. If I listed every single thing you've done for me, I'd be here till next Christmas."

Kris hugged him, but George didn't return it. He could feel himself sliding into one of his dissociative attacks. Kris's words were far from reassuring to him, but he was just about with it enough to remember he was supposed to focus on something outside of himself and caught sight of the flashing lights on the antler headband, homing in on them and watching the LEDs chase around and around.

"George?" Kris hadn't seen him have a seizure before and panicked, unaware that Josh was standing a few feet away and immediately recognised what was happening.

"It's OK," Josh said. "Just stay where you are, Kris." Josh slowly moved into the room and knelt in front of the sofa. "That's it. Keep watching those lights, George. What kinds of patterns do they make? It looks a bit like a heart to me."

Kris tried to maintain his breathing and stay completely still, but he was starting to hyperventilate.

Without taking his eyes off George, Josh reached across and held Kris's hand. "It's OK," he repeated. "I heard a little of what you said, and it'll have worried him."

"Why? I was telling him how important he is to me."

"I know, but it kind of sounded like, erm…" Josh did a quick rephrase. "Like you were saying goodbye."

"Oh!" Kris recoiled in horror. "No, George. Oh, God. That's what Dan thought too. I didn't mean that at all, George. I'm not going anywhere, I promise. I just needed you to know that I was sorry for not being a good friend. Hey, I'll even let you tell me I'm confused if you—"

George blinked a couple of times.

"There you go," Josh said. He placed Kris's hand on top of George's. "Nearly back now." He glanced at Kris. "You're going to be in so much trouble when he comes round."

"I don't care!" Kris said.

George squeezed his hand. "Confused," he slurred.

Kris looked into his eyes and smiled in an attempt to disguise how worried he still was.

George did his best to smile in return. He hadn't properly come out of the seizure yet, although it was minor, and he was completely aware of his surroundings. It felt a little like being underwater and trying to push up to the surface, but he was definitely getting better at managing them. The fact he was trying to compare the experience to something else told him that and also gave him a last foot-up. He nodded at Kris.

"I'm OK."

Kris let out a long, deep breath. "You scared me."

"You scared me first."

"I'm sorry. I didn't mean—"

"Oy! Superstar!"

The words were hollered from the hallway, and Kris gulped, knowing that it was George's mum, and that she was talking to him.

"Get yer arse out 'ere. NOW!"

Kris looked to Josh for instruction, but Josh merely nodded and said, "I'll stay with George."

The two men exchanged places, and Josh whispered, "Good luck!"

Kris glanced back gloomily and passed Shaunna in the doorway.

Shaunna quickly sat on the chair and flinched as the kitchen door slammed shut, not that it made any difference. They could hear every word, as, no doubt, could the girl upstairs and quite possibly the rest of the terrace.

***

"Right, lad, what's all this about you and Shaunna?"

"What's that, Iris?" Kris asked innocently.

"Don't come all butter wouldn't melt with me. You bin fuckin' about with that feller of yours under her roof and keepin' her from leavin'!"

"That's not quite how—"

"That's exactly how it friggin' well is, and you know it. So, what you doin' about it?"

"Well, I—"

"I'll tell you what you're goin' to do. For starters, you can stop bloody apologisin' left, right and centre and grow a pair o' balls. So you had a perv for an uncle? Everyone has a fucker like that lurkin' somewhere in the family. See that littlun upstairs? Her mam and dad…" Iris shook her head, her eyes ablaze with anger. "An' all you've got to worry about is some old bastard who's probably long dead."

Kris looked at the floor and kept looking at it whilst Iris continued to give him what could only be described as a bollocking.

"You arty-farty lot and all your deep and meaningfuls…what a load of shite that is. You're not a bloody mess because of your uncle, you're a bloody mess because you think someone's goin' to keep pickin' you up and mollycoddlin' yer. Them lot in there an' the rest of 'em? You've no idea just how lucky you are, lad, to have friends like them, but they must've had it to the back teeth with your whinin'."

Kris was still staring at the floor, following the grout trail around the tiles to distract himself from the brutality of the truth Iris was delivering. He was on the brink of bursting into tears, holding it in for fear of getting a smack around the head. His parents weren't soft, but they'd never given him a telling-off like this.

It was a bit odd, really, to think he'd turn forty in a few weeks, and here he was, getting an ear bashing that he hoped would end soon, of course, yet it kind of felt good because Iris was right. He deserved it. More than that, he knew she was doing it because she cared about him. Everyone else had been pussyfooting around him, saying what he thought he needed to hear, but *this* was what he really needed.

He glanced up at her through his eyelashes and smiled sheepishly. She folded her arms.

"Nowt about it's your fault, lad, right?"

He shrugged. Not his fault; he was working on that one.

"And you've made a start by sayin' you're sorry, but I'll tell you now. You do anythin' to upset Shaunna or Georgie or anyone else again, an' I'll have your guts for garters. D'you hear?"

Kris nodded.

"Good. Now come 'ere." She grabbed him and hauled him in, giving him a tight, motherly hug, which naturally made him bawl like a baby. "It's all right, lad," she said gently. That made him cry all the more, and she kept hold of him until he found he could stop, then she kissed him on the forehead.

"You're a bloody daft bugger, you," she said, ruffling his hair. "I hope that feller of yours has got his head screwed on."

"He has," Kris sniffed.

"And d'you love him?"

"Yes."

"Then make each other happy, love. Simple as that."

She ripped a length of paper towel from the roll, shoved it in his hand, sent him back to the lounge, and took herself outside for a cigarette.

***

89

Josh moved so Kris could sit down again, and he flopped into the sofa, battle-weary and more than a little shell-shocked.

"Kris, I'm really—" George started, but Kris grabbed his hand and stopped him mid-flow.

"I love your mum, George," he said. "She's bloody wonderful, but can I have my beer now, please?"

10. Sleighride

THE MOTORWAY TO Manchester was surprisingly clear, and they made good time, arriving at Ade's sister's house a little after four o'clock. The sky was turning dark and slowly filling with stars; a crisp-edged crescent moon glowed just above the line of frost-glistened rooftops. Andy got out of the car and started unloading bags and cases from the boot. Kris went to lend a hand. He deposited his own and Ade's bags at the end of the driveway and returned to the car.

"Thanks for the lift," he said.

Andy glanced sideways at him. "Well, you were pretty insistent!"

Kris grinned and held out his hand, preparing for the exchange. "You did bring yours, didn't you?"

Andy covered his mouth as if he'd forgotten, but then pulled his passport from his pocket, along with a set of keys. Kris went to take the keys from him, but Andy put an arm around him and hauled him in for a hug.

"I'm glad we're sorted," Andy said. "We've known each other a long time, and your friendship is too important to lose. I would've bowed out, you know."

"I know." Kris was truly humbled by Andy's words. "Thank you. For everything."

Andy released him. "Likewise. So, you gonna tell me where we're going?"

Kris delved inside his jacket and withdrew a well-stuffed envelope. "It's all in here. Boarding passes, luggage tags, hotel reservation, equipment hire. Plane takes off in two hours and ten minutes, so you'll be there in time to leave a cookie and milk for Santa."

Andy opened the envelope and flicked through the contents. They were all as Kris had described and related to a three-night break at a ski and snowboarding resort.

"Kris, mate…"

A taxi pulled into the cul-de-sac.

"That's yours," Kris said. "I'll get Ade to move the Mustang into Julia's garage once we're done here." He placed Shaunna's passport on top of Andy's and held out his hand for the keys to the Mustang. Andy tried to give the envelope back instead. Kris pushed it away. "It's the least I can do. I know it's not Canada…"

"Switzerland's not cheap."

"No, but it's only money, and I had a bit of a windfall, so just get in your taxi before you freeze your bits and bobs off. I have a feeling you might be needing them tonight."

Andy relented. "Thanks, then." He handed over his keys. "Don't let him prang it, will you?"

"Don't you worry. I'm well experienced in looking after your girls."

Andy shook his head. "Krissi will always be your girl, and as for her mother…" He peered through the Mustang's rear window at Shaunna, who was watching them both carefully. "She belongs to no-one."

"But she does belong *with* you—in Switzerland, so scoot!"

Andy laughed. "Have a good one, yeah?"

"We will."

Kris waited for Andy and Shaunna to transfer their luggage and themselves to the taxi and signalled to Julia inside the house. She switched on her outside Christmas lights, which had previously consisted of an understated chain of icicles along the guttering and some fairy lights on a tree but now included four illuminated reindeer attached to the strangest looking sleigh, as it wasn't a sleigh at all. It was a Jaguar E-Type in British racing green—Ade's dream car—which Andy had arranged the purchase of on Kris's behalf. Kris took Ade by the hand and led him past the reindeer, dangling the keys in front of him.

Ade looked at the keys and then at the Jaguar. "You didn't!" he said. "You…how did you do this?" He threw his arms around Kris and kissed him. "This is amazing, and you are totally nuts, but I love you." He kissed him again. "Thank you, although it's far too expensive. I can't possibly keep it."

"Yes, you can. The network gagged me."

"They paid you off?"

"Yep. I'm done with *Shadows* for good. 'New Year, New Me', as they say." Kris smiled cheesily.

"You do realise my present for you is totally crap compared to this?"

Kris shrugged. "Do you promise not to throw up on me if I tell you I've already got what I want?"

Ade mimed throwing up, and Kris rolled his eyes.

"See, nobody ever believes I'm being sincere."

"Try it again."

Kris took both of Ade's hands and looked into his eyes, trying to keep his expression serious. "All I want for Christmas is you," he said. Ade burst out laughing. "OK, I give up."

They heard a diesel engine start behind them and stopped playing silly games to wave Andy and Shaunna off. Shaunna wound down the window, and Kris went over. He reached in and kissed her gently.

"Have an amazing Christmas, wife-ex-wife."

She smiled up at him and cupped his cheek in her palm. "You too, husband-ex-husband."

Kris stepped back and watched as the taxi completed a circle and slowly rolled out of the cul-de-sac.

Ade hooked his arm through Kris's. "The E-Type is fab, but that—" he nodded after the departing tail lights "—is the best present you could ever have given me."

"Don't tell me you want a snowboarding holiday too?" Kris joked, but he knew what Ade meant. He'd finally made the break from Shaunna and in doing so cemented his commitment to Ade. He indicated the Jaguar. "Did you want to take it out for a spin?"

"I think I'd rather wait for daylight, if that's OK with you?"

"Of course! It's your car."

"I know, but I don't want you to think I'm not excited about it, because I am. Far too excited to drive sensibly in this weather." Ade noticed Kris was shivering and extended his coat around him. "We should go inside."

"Good idea."

They started walking towards the house.

"Didn't you want to ask me something?" Ade said.

"Err…" Kris stopped walking. "Yeah. I do, but it's a bit—" He blew steamy breath slowly from his mouth, trying to think of a good way to put it. There wasn't one. "When we're, you know… and I'm, err…"

"Yes?" Ade said, trying not to laugh at Kris's awkwardness.

"Well, is the yelling because I'm hurting you, or—" Ade silenced him with a kiss.

"No, it's not," he assured him earnestly. "You've caused me a lot of pain this last year, babe, but not that way."

"You would tell me, wouldn't you? If you didn't want to—"

This time, Kris stopped because Ade pulled away from him. Kris put his head down, ashamed that he needed to ask the question. He should be able to read the signals.

Ade tugged at Kris's sleeve until he got his attention and stared deep into his eyes, past the façade of performance they both used as a safety blanket, searching out the real Kristian Johansson—the loving, vulnerable boy who had hidden away in his own world of make-believe—not of fairy-tale princes and happily-ever-afters, but a nightmare of misunderstanding and measuring intimacy against the standards set by his abuser.

Ade held his gaze, waiting for Kris to let him in, the smallest sigh the only outward sign he had done so.

"I love you," Kris said quietly.

Ade nodded. "I believe you, but if you don't talk to someone about this, it's going to destroy us too."

"I'm scared."

"Yes, but I'm going to be with you all the way, I promise. Now, are you ready to go in? Because I am absolutely bloody frozen!"

Kris allowed Ade to lead him by the hand to the front door, which flew open as they approached.

"At last! I thought you'd both turned to ice!" Julia ushered them inside.

"Not far off!" Ade said, putting his very cold hands on his sister's hot cheeks and making her jump.

"Well, you're just in time for a glass of mulled wine. That'll soon defrost you."

They set aside the rest of it for later and stepped into the welcoming warmth of a family Christmas.

***

"So," Shaunna said as soon as the safety belt light went out. "Mile High Club?" She walked her fingers up the inside of Andy's thigh. He slapped them still before they reached their destination.

"No way!"

She glanced around the almost empty cabin. "No-one'll know."

Andy shook his head. "D'you think they might have security cameras on planes these days?"

"I thought you liked the idea of getting caught in the act."

"I don't like the idea of starring in *Caught on Camera*!"

Shaunna giggled. "I can see it now," she said. She braced her shoulders, stuck out her chest and said in a deep voice, "Adele? Come and look at this. Do those arse cheeks look familiar?"

Andy laughed. He reached over and kissed her. "Patience, my red-hot baby. You'll just have to wait till we get to the hotel."

"Damn." Shaunna sat back in her seat and leaned against Andy's shoulder. "I can't believe Kris did this for us."

"I know. He's awesome."

"And still scary?"

"Nah."

Shaunna leaned forward and examined the bulge in Andy's jeans. She licked her lips and flashed him a seductive smile. "Then that must be for me." She put her free hand on his knee, and he captured it immediately.

"Later!"

"Spoilsport."

He turned and kissed her head. "It'll be worth the wait, I promise."

"How about a taster?" she suggested, turning her face towards his. He moved closer and kissed her—a long, slow kiss that went on for many minutes, her tongue in his mouth, then his tongue in hers, the desire gradually building in both of them to a point where it was almost impossible to stop, and they eased away from each other breathlessly.

"More of those, please," Andy said, closing his eyes and trying to ignore the gentle brush of her thumb against the throbbing in his jeans. She smiled and moved her hand away, but not without increasing the pressure first. He drew back.

"If I last a minute when we get to the hotel, I'll be lucky."

"You need that long?" She exhaled very slowly and relaxed into her seat, settling in for the remaining hour of their flight.

***

'Hotel' wasn't an entirely accurate description of the place Kris had booked, in that it was more of a holiday village, with its own ski school and various other winter sports amenities, set on a mini plateau up in the mountains. The building outside which their taxi stopped was a grand-looking chalet built on various levels cut into the mountainside, with multiple roofs covered in snow and small white bulbs around their facing gable ends. The left side of the chalet was obscured by thick evergreens adorned with brightly coloured lights, and an orange glow illuminated every window, spilling out across the snow, down towards an ice rink that was possibly a frozen lake.

"It's like a Thomas Kinkade painting," Shaunna said, awestruck by the beauty of the place.

Andy wasn't looking at the building; he was looking at the woman standing next to him, drawn moth-like to the flaming halo of light illuminating her glorious red tresses, loose spirals framing cheeks turned rosy-pink by the ice-cold evening, the wisps of hot breath misting the air around her and making her look altogether ethereal, an angel. His angel. He was gone.

Wondering why he was so quiet, Shaunna turned and caught him watching her—no mistaking what was on his mind. He coughed, embarrassed.

"Thomas Kinkade?" he repeated to prove he'd been listening. "Related to Mrs. K.?" He was referring to their old primary school teacher, although Andy was the only one hard-faced enough to call her that and also the only one who could get away with it.

"I doubt it," Shaunna replied, "although you never know. Didn't she say she studied art?"

"No idea." Much as the view was beautiful—his and hers— the wind was bitter and their bags were heavy, but Andy had insisted on carrying them both. He waited for Shaunna to pick up her handbag—a huge, hand-woven satchel he'd brought back from Nepal on his first visit over ten years ago. He didn't say so, but he was overjoyed she still had it and was using it. It wasn't a lot lighter than the luggage, but she slung it effortlessly over her shoulder. Awestruck as usual, he followed her up the steps into the hotel.

"Ms. Hennessy and Mr. Jeffries," a smiling middle-aged man in an open-necked shirt and chunky beige cardigan greeted them.

"Err, yes," Shaunna confirmed, surprised by the personal address. The man turned and spoke in French to the only other person in sight—a younger man of no more than twenty-five—and then turned back to Shaunna and Andy.

"Gabe will show you to your chalet."

"*Our* chalet?"

"The gentleman who called said you needed your privacy, and I can appreciate why."

Shaunna frowned. "Why?"

"I recognised you as soon as you stepped out of the taxi, Ms. Hennessy, or should I say, Mrs. Johansson?"

"Ah." *Shadows* strikes again. Thankfully, it didn't happen very often, but Shaunna had been caught with Kris—and without—by the paparazzi enough times to be recognised by his fans, of which, it seemed, the hotel owner was one. He was barely containing his excitement at the conclusion he had reached of his own accord.

"Was it he who made the booking?" he asked. "I did send him an email many months ago, offering our accommodations. Of course, he must get a great number of messages like that." He smiled hopefully at Shaunna. She nodded.

"Yes, it was Kristian who called, Monsieur…?"

"Lustenberger. Leon Lustenberger, but it is a comical name to the English, is it not?"

Shaunna giggled. "Maybe if you didn't point it out, people wouldn't notice?"

He bowed his head in acceptance. "Please, call me Leon," he beseeched, smiling warmly again. Shaunna decided she liked him.

"Ms. Hennessy? Are you coming?" Andy called from the other side of the lobby, where he was waiting with Gabe.

"It's lovely to meet you, Leon," she said, going to shake the man's hand, but instead, he gently lifted her hand and kissed it.

"For me also." He released her, and she floated away on the wave of flattery.

"Sorry," she said to Andy, blushing as they stepped out into the cold once more. "He's a paid-up member of the Kristian Johansson fan club."

"I got that." Gabe had put their bags on a trolley and was pulling it along in front of them. Andy put his arm around Shaunna's shoulders. "Though I think he's probably more of a Shaunna Johansson fan myself."

"Jealous?"

"Me? Nah. They can look as much as they like."

She peered up at him, and he grinned. Yes, he loved that men thought his woman was hot, and it made her feel pretty special too.

"Here we are," Gabe said, drawing up outside a miniature version of the hotel. He took a key from his body-warmer pocket, opened the door for them and started to unload their bags.

"I'll deal with those, mate," Andy offered.

"As you wish." Gabe set the bags down outside the door and folded his trolley.

"Wow!" Shaunna peered inside and then stepped back to take in the outside again. "When I hear 'chalet' I always picture those dodgy prefabs we used to stay in at Pontins, not a cosy log cabin in the mountains."

"Leo…err, Herr Lustenberger asked that I set the fire for you. Should you need more logs or anything else, call through to the reception and I will be glad to assist you."

Andy gave him a thumbs up.

Gabe nodded once and swiftly departed, leaving them to get acquainted with their accommodation for the next three days.

Andy put his arms around Shaunna from behind and snuffed in her hair. "I'd offer to carry you over the threshold, but…"

"Now why would you do that?"

"Well, it's kind of our first home together."

Shaunna shook her hair in his face, and he loosened his grip for her to turn to face him. "Sometimes you are hopelessly romantic." He blinked at her beseechingly. She sighed. "Go on then."

He didn't need telling twice. Scooping her up in his arms, he set off, skidding on the compacted snow and only just righting himself as they staggered sideways through the doorway, both of them laughing. He gently set her on her feet again and pulled her close, gazing lovingly at her...until he spotted the salopettes hanging in the corner of the room, the edge of a snowboard peeking out from behind.

Shaunna turned to see what had distracted him. "So I'm sharing you this holiday?" she said.

Andy tried to push away the feelings of guilt and disappointment that her question had evoked. However, he couldn't see her face, and when she turned back, he found she was smiling. "I can't wait to see you on a snowboard."

"Really?"

"Oh, yeah! And I'd love for you to teach me if there's time."

He kissed her again, and this time, he didn't get distracted. "I didn't think I could love you more than I already did."

She raised an eyebrow and leaned into him. "Yep, there's definitely some big love going on down there."

"I'm gonna bring the bags in and shower first," he said.

"OK. I'll have a nosey around, see what drinks they've provided us with. I bet there's no tea."

She crossed the chalet to the kitchen area, peering inside the cupboards to see what was on offer, discovering it was quite well stocked, with packets of biscuits and a few tins of food, plus milk, coffee and teabags. There was also real hot chocolate and marshmallows, and she wondered how much of it was part of the standard package and how much Kris had asked the hotel to provide as added extras. She opted for the hot chocolate and filled a small pan with milk, using the time it took to heat to further explore the chalet.

It was of an open-plan design, the only exception being the bathroom, which ran alongside the kitchenette, both rooms taking up around a third of the available space. The remaining two-thirds contained a king-size bed and a large sofa draped with blankets, where Andy deposited their bags on his way to the bathroom. Between the sofa and the fire was a fluffy rug, and a little Christmas tree had been erected next to the hearth. Shaunna closed the curtains on the small windows either side of the fireplace, glancing briefly at the total darkness outside, and went to make the hot chocolate.

She took the cups over to the sofa and sat, listening to Andy singing to himself in the shower. 'I Wish It Could Be Christmas Everyday'—an apt choice, all considered, but she was feeling tired and fidgety. She got up again and went to inspect the bed.

Often, that was the major let-down. The accommodation would be beautiful, the food fantastic, but the bed would be rock solid with springs sticking up all over the place and feather pillows that didn't hold their shape, not that she agreed with feather pillows, anyway. On this occasion, however, she was delighted to find that the plush, linen-covered pillows were of the hollow-fibre variety, and the mattress was, as Goldilocks would say, 'just right'. She lay on her side and let out a deep, gratifying sigh.

***

A minute or so later, Andy emerged from the bathroom with a towel draped around his waist, expecting to have it whipped off. When that didn't happen, he glanced over to the bed, where Shaunna was curled up, her hands clasped beneath her cheek, already fast asleep. Andy pulled on a pair of shorts and slurped at the hot chocolate she'd made, not sure if she'd want him to wake her so she could drink hers, but she looked so peaceful he couldn't bring himself to disturb her. Instead, he grabbed the blankets from the sofa rather than try to extract the duvet from underneath her. He lay next to her and covered them both.

***

She woke a little after three a.m., desperate for the loo and slightly disoriented, as well as annoyed she'd fallen asleep. When she returned from the bathroom, Andy was under the duvet. She took off everything except her knickers and T-shirt and climbed in beside him, resting her head on his chest.

"Sorry," she whispered.

"It's OK." He put his arms around her and kissed her head. "It'll wait till morning."

11. Christmas Present

S EVEN THIRTY, CHRISTMAS morning: Andy woke first, which was how it should be, he'd come to realise through the very occasional night together they'd snatched during the past two and a half months. He wasn't an early riser as such, but Shaunna liked to lie in, which today afforded him time to see what the situation was with breakfast. He felt like it was taking liberties to call through to reception, given what day it was, so he pulled on last night's clothes, grabbed the chalet key and left, quietly closing the door behind him.

The world was still silently sleeping, awaiting first light, and the peace was incredible yet strangely unnerving. It was a long time since he'd walked alone through snow-covered mountains, even if he could now make out other chalets dotted all around. Up ahead of him, the main hotel complex rose out of the snow, a shimmering beacon of white and gold.

"Their electricity bill must be through the roof," Andy thought aloud, crunching his way along the coarsely gritted path, taking great care to wipe his feet as he stepped inside the overly warm lobby.

"Good morning, Mr. Jeffries," Gabe greeted him cheerily.

"Alright?" Andy replied with a grin.

"And a very Merry Christmas to you," Gabe added.

"Cheers. And to you."

"Were you warm enough?"

"Absolutely. The chalet's excellent."

"I'm pleased to hear it."

"You been here all night?"

"Yes, but it was quiet and I was able to study."

Andy was impressed by Gabe's ability to be so full of beans when he'd had no sleep. He even looked freshly groomed, with his goatee beard cutting sharp angles against his stubble-less chin. Gabe continued to smile, and Andy realised he was staring. He coughed nervously. "What're you studying?" he asked. He was expecting an answer along the lines of philosophy or ancient history.

"Accounting," Gabe said. "Herr Lustenberger is footing the bill."

"Cool." Andy nodded, not really knowing what else to say.

Gabe waited a moment longer before prompting, "How can I be of assistance?"

"Ah, yeah. I came to find out how breakfast works?"

"We serve breakfast in the restaurant from eight until ten, but I can arrange for it to be brought over to your chalet, if you wish."

"That's a lot of hassle," Andy said, although it was his preferred option.

"Not at all, Mr. Jeffries. Herr Lustenberger is eager to ensure that Ms. Hennessy enjoys some privacy."

"I'll bet he is," Andy muttered under his breath. Gabe didn't quite catch it and smiled attentively, perhaps hoping Andy would repeat himself. "You're sure it's no problem?" Andy asked instead.

"We have quite a few guests staying for the festive period, so please do not worry about making the most of your time here." Gabe reached under the counter and retrieved a breakfast menu. Andy took it from him and scanned the list of items, each given in several languages, including English.

"These are German breakfasts," he observed.

"Yes. Most local people eat only bread and jam, but Herr Lustenberger is German himself, and our guests appreciate a more substantial start to their day, so we have bread, cured meats and cheeses. The yoghurt is very nice also."

Andy pondered. It struck him that he actually had no idea what Shaunna liked for breakfast, although he wouldn't have been at all surprised to discover it was just a cup of tea.

"Perhaps I could send a selection over, with tea and coffee?" Gabe suggested.

Andy nodded. "That'd be awesome, cheers." He passed back the menu.

"I'll bring it across to you as soon as the kitchen staff is ready. About eight fifteen?"

Andy nodded again to confirm the arrangement and headed back outside, where it was starting to get light, giving him his first tantalising glimpse of the mountains. He felt the tingle of adrenaline surge through his arms and legs and smiled. Even if he only got out there for a couple of hours, it would be paradise. He hadn't been boarding for a good few years, and the prospect of doing so and then coming home to someone made him feel on top of the world. Or on top of the Alps, at any rate.

He arrived back at the chalet and let himself in, pausing to watch Shaunna, still asleep and as beautiful as ever. Time for a quick shower before breakfast arrived. Then he would wake her, or that was his plan. However, when he emerged from the bathroom, this time wearing one of the complimentary bathrobes, she was already awake.

"Good morning, RHB," he said, bending down to kiss her. She gave him a wicked grin and tugged open the bathrobe, which was exactly what he'd anticipated.

"Well, hello there!" she said, eyeing the red ribbon tied in a bow around her first 'Christmas present' of the day.

"A word of warning," Andy said, his voice rising a little as she gripped one end of the ribbon with her lips. "If you're intending to open that now, you've got about ten minutes before breakfast arrives."

"Ten minutes?" she repeated incredulously. "As if it's going to take ten minutes!" She moved to the side of the bed and grabbed the ribbon again, gently tugging at it until the bow started to loosen. Andy chanced a glance downwards just as she took the longer of the two ends of ribbon and nibbled her way to its point of origin, her lips making contact with flesh. Far too erotic. He closed his eyes, focusing on the sensation of the tug on the ribbon and her breath against him.

"You gone off my hair this morning?" Shaunna asked.

He shook his head. With what she was doing, one touch would probably finish him completely, and he didn't want that, for him or for her.

She continued to alternate her attention between untying the bow and play-biting what it was attached to, the desire mounting within her to the point where she wanted to take him entirely in her mouth, but she didn't want it to end yet either. Then she hit on a snag.

"Ah," she said. "It's…" She frowned and examined the ribbon. "There's a knot in it."

"Yeah, it's getting a bit tight."

"I'll see if I can untie it." She picked at the knot with her fingernails, but it was wet and very tight, and the loop was starting to dig into him. She shook her head. "It's no use. I'm going to have to cut it off."

Andy wobbled and staggered backwards. It wasn't an act. "Cut it off?" he repeated.

"The ribbon," she clarified.

"I figured. With what?"

"Scissors." She went over to the kitchenette and rooted through the drawers in search of a pair but couldn't locate any. She did, however, find a vegetable knife. She took it back to the bed.

"Oh, no!" Andy backed off.

"It'll be fine. I'll—"

"No way are you bringing that knife anywhere near my—"

"I'll just slide the blade under the ribbon. It's pretty sharp."

The colour drained from Andy's face, although a certain other body part was turning a nice shade of plum purple.

"Sharp is better," Shaunna reasoned. "It'll slice straight through. Otherwise I'd have to saw at it."

"Maybe we could just wait a while?"

"I hate to tell you, hun, but you ain't gonna go soft any time soon." She moved a step closer.

Andy gulped, absolutely terrified.

"I'll be really careful," she promised. "After all, it'd be a *huge* loss to both of us."

He continued to stare at her, horrified and helpless. She nodded to reassure him. After a further few seconds of willing his erection to go down—without success—he accepted he had no choice and shrugged in submission.

"Of course," she said, advancing on him with the knife, "it was a bit silly tying a ribbon around it to begin with." She eased the point of the blade under the tight loop. "But thanks. This is definitely the most fun I've ever had playing with a Christmas present." She glanced up and blew him a kiss. His eyes widened.

"Could you concentrate on what you're doing?"

She sighed in exasperation and continued to wiggle the knife, the flat of the blade now in between him and the ribbon. She twisted the knife to the side, finally gaining some leverage, when there was a knock at the door. She jumped, and her hand jolted. Andy nearly fainted.

"Damn. So close." She left the knife where it was and stood up. "Stay there," she commanded and went to answer the door.

"Good morning." Gabe smiled at her.

"Good morning, and Merry Christmas," she said brightly, as if she hadn't just been trying to free an engorged manhood from a tightly knotted red ribbon.

"And to you, Ms. Hennessy. Would you like me to bring the tray inside for you?"

She glanced back at Andy. He was holding his breath, and the bathrobe in front of him. "It's fine. I can take it from here," she said.

Gabe nodded politely and turned away. She started to close the door.

"Oh, Ms. Hennessy? Herr Lustenberger said I was to inform you that there is a news item about your husband on the internet this morning."

"OK, thank you." She closed the door and carried the tray over to the bed. It was amazing how blasé she had become about the media's fabrications and exaggerations of what Kris had said or done, but it was at least a weekly occurrence and a normal part of their lives. Nevertheless, she could appreciate its novelty for other people, particularly as she was here with another man.

She set the tray down and returned to her previous task, which was no easier for the interlude, as Andy was more swollen than before and the knife was jammed up against him. It was also starting to get a little painful, so he didn't protest at all this time, desperate to be free.

"There you go." Shaunna held up the severed ribbon as evidence. Andy sighed in relief and flopped back onto the bed, spread-eagled, stark naked and not caring in the slightest. Shaunna reached over and kissed him on the chin. "Give it a good rub to get the blood flowing again while I pop to the bathroom. Be right back."

She was only gone long enough to use the loo and brush her teeth, but by the time she'd returned, the fire was roaring, and Andy, now in board shorts, was casually sitting, cross-legged, in the middle of the bed with the breakfast tray in front of him and his phone in his hand. Shaunna climbed onto the bed and mirrored his pose.

"Mmm. Smells delicious," she said, eyeing him over. He gave her that coy smile he had, where one corner of his mouth went up more than the other, leaving a dimple in his cheek. She lingered on the vision and the accompanying thoughts a moment longer and then lifted one of the plate covers.

"Before you eat, you need to see this," he said, holding out his phone.

She took it and scanned the screen, her frown slowly transforming into an expression of disbelief. "Oh, for God's sake!"

"Do you want to call him?"

She nodded. "Yeah. Better had."

She passed his phone back for him to make the call. "Hey, Kris."

"Good morning. Happy Christmas!"

"And to you, mate. I'll just hand you over." He gave the phone to Shaunna again.

"Hiya. Merry Christmas, hun. Have you seen it?"

"Yeah, but we knew it was coming. We saw a camera flash when we were moving the Mustang into the garage."

"Are you OK?"

"'Course! Are you?"

"Well, yeah." Shaunna poked at the bread on the plate, trying to word what she wanted to say. "It would've been nice if we'd had the chance to get used to it ourselves first, though. Are you sure you're OK?"

"I'm fine, honestly."

She heard music start up in the background. "It sounds like you're having fun. Have you opened your present from Ade yet?" It was a leather-bound special edition of Shakespeare's Sonnets, and Ade had been fretting over his choice for weeks.

"I have," Kris said. "It's beautiful, although I haven't had a chance to look at it properly."

The music became louder, accompanied by several voices singing just as loudly, followed by Ade yelling, "Merry Christmas," into the phone. Shaunna moved it away from her ear so both of them could listen to the noisy celebration at the other end of the line.

"It's mental here," Kris explained, unnecessarily. "I'm gonna go. Have a wonderful Christmas. You deserve the best."

Shaunna felt a lump rise in her throat and swallowed it down. "Love to you and Ade," she said quickly and hung up. A tear escaped, and she laughed at herself, still nursing the phone and fighting the urge to cry.

Andy reached across and wiped the tear away with his thumb. "OK?"

She nodded, and it was the truth. For twenty-four years, she and Kris had spent Christmas together, and she was sad it was over. Yet, at the same time, here she was, in a cosy, romantic Swiss chalet with Andy, and she knew without a doubt that it was what she wanted. She gave him a smile. "I'm a bit emotional, that's all."

"How's Kris taking it?"

"He's fine." In fact, she was surprised at how well he had taken it. Along with a photo of Ade reversing the Mustang into his sister's garage, the press had somehow got a shot of Shaunna and Andy smooching in the airport and stuck a headline over both, declaring 'Johansson's Dreams In Tatters', with a stream of poison about him being 'sacked' from *Shadows* and a damning indictment of his personal life that wasn't far off the truth, but quite how they'd found out about the web of relationships was anyone's guess.

"Shall I pour the tea?" Andy suggested.

"Good idea." She attempted to cast it from her mind, but it wasn't easy, and she was starting to worry that there might be journalists lurking around the hotel. Maybe they'd paid off Leon so they could scoop an exclusive on 'Johansson's wife and her bit on the side'. No, she was being paranoid. Leon seemed sincere in wanting to protect her from prying eyes, and in any case, Andy was more than capable of seeing off trouble. *Bit on the side.*

How funny. And how incredible. They were officially a couple. The thought gave her butterflies and a whole lot more besides.

"Are you gonna eat?" Andy asked, pulling her out of the rather dirty trajectory her thoughts had taken. She piled some cheese onto a slice of bread and took a hearty bite, giving her lips a slow lick as she watched Andy watching her.

They both ate in silence until they'd had their fill, their lack of enthusiasm no reflection on the food. The breakfast was tasty, but theirs was a different hunger, and as soon as they were done, Andy shoved the tray to the bottom of the bed and pushed Shaunna onto her back, slowly lowering his face until their lips met, increasing the pressure of the kiss, pausing only so they could remove each other's scant clothing.

He moved against her as she lifted her legs, and he fell between them into that natural, irrepressible locking together of their bodies. Her back arched, and she tilted her pelvis, pushing him deeper, eyes closed, mouth open, breath momentarily suspended.

"You're so beautiful," he murmured.

She let the breath go and grunted a little. "More action," she ordered.

He obediently set to it, taking it slowly, his intention to build up speed gradually and make it last. Shaunna had other ideas and moved faster, throwing them out of sync.

"More," she gasped.

"More?" he asked a little smugly because for once, he was pretty sure he had more to give. He wasn't going to get away with teasing her for long, he knew that, but it was worth pushing it just to watch her bucking against him and her breasts jiggling with the motion.

"So help me..." she growled, grabbing him by the buttocks and attempting to pull him tight against her, but she was no match for those muscles. Even so, he decided to give her what she wanted.

Propping himself up on his arms, he tightened his abs and continued his rhythmic thrusting, her movements matching his. He looked down over her body, following the silky curve of her breasts, her peachy nipples large and erect, her perfectly round, soft belly, the arrow-head of red hair pointing to where they were joined, and took a moment to proudly admire the power of his thigh muscles rippling, his body penetrating hers.

She hooked his chin with her finger and brought his attention back to her face, lifting herself from the bed so she could reach that glorious cleft chin, doing her usual flick of the tongue, trying to kiss him in between panting and moaning.

She was on the edge, he could feel it, and he eased back, knowing her response would be to pull him down on top of her in her search for release. He lifted a hand and cupped her head, tangling his fingers in her hair, and resumed his previous rhythm, working his lower body to push deeper and deeper inside her, each subsequent thrust eliciting a louder groan than the last, until he felt her muscles tense around him, and then it was like fireworks erupting in his head as two days of teasing rewarded him with an enormous, intense orgasm. It felt as if his groin was on fire, and it seemed to go on and on.

They finally collapsed onto the bed, and Shaunna pushed him so that he rolled onto his side, still kissing with a furious passion, riding the afterglow.

"That'll be the ribbon," she said breathlessly.

"Huh?"

"Cutting off the circulation. More time to build up to it."

"Ah." Now he appreciated the purpose of some of the male sex aids he'd seen on his travels. He'd been told they enhanced performance and was glad to say he'd never needed to enhance his, but that was before he'd lain down with his relentless red-hot baby. Perhaps it was time for a rethink.

Reality gradually returned around them…the warm, flickering glow of the fireplace…the lingering scent of tea and sex.

Shaunna got up and went to shower. Andy threw another log on the fire and made hot chocolate. She returned from the bathroom and made a beeline for Andy's bag, from which she extracted a large, chunky jumper. It was bright red with a polar bear on the front. She put it on, along with a pair of knickers, grabbed his present from her own bag and went to join him on the sofa, where he was nursing his present for her.

"I wish I'd brought a clip with me." She flicked her wet hair back over her shoulders. It was already getting on her nerves.

Andy reached behind him and then brought his arm back into view. "Like this one?"

She examined the large sprung claw clip on his upturned palm.

"I figured, seeing as I broke the last one..."

"Yeah, you did." She took it from him and scooped up her hair. "Thanks."

"It's got a titanium spring," he explained, watching her fight to squeeze the clip open.

"Just as well!"

With her hair secured—for now—they exchanged their gifts and both immediately ripped off all the paper.

"Ha!" Andy beat her by milliseconds. "These are awesome!" He opened the box and tipped the contents onto the sofa: finger extreme sports, consisting of a mini BMX, skateboard and ramp, complete with spare wheels, extra decks and a couple of tiny wrenches. He put his fingers on top of the skateboard and ran it along the back of the sofa, grinding a cushion and performing a frontside 180 as he came to land on her knee. She stopped fighting with the box containing her own present to applaud his efforts. He grinned and 'fell off' his skateboard, but it wasn't a bad fall and he walked away—with his fingers—all the way up her thigh, kissed her tenderly in thanks and sat back so she could open her present.

"I need that knife again," Shaunna said, getting up to retrieve it. Andy gulped loudly, and she started giggling. "Just for the sticky tape," she assured him. She slit the tape all along the end of the box and at last pulled her present free: a miniature tabletop football game. "Oh, this is too cool," she said, bouncing up and down in delight. Given that she wasn't wearing a bra, it was quite a delight for Andy too.

"I hope that's OK," he hedged, even though her reaction said it all. "There's not much to choose from when you're looking for something small that doesn't cost a lot. If you'd just said small, I'd have known exactly what to get you."

"Neither of your gifts are small, though, are they?" Shaunna reached over and ran a fingertip down from his belly button, over the waistband of his shorts, all the way along the seam. Andy's eyelids lilted. She laughed again and kissed him. "It's perfect," she said, "and I'm totally gonna kick your ass at it later."

"Says you!"

"You know it!"

She set the table football to one side so she could snuggle up against him. He passed her a cup of hot chocolate and put his arm around her. "So," she said, "do we have plans for the rest of the day?"

"Just take it as it comes, I reckon."

"Sounds good."

A few more minutes passed in silence but for the crackling of the fire and occasional contented sighs from one or the other of them.

"I've got another present for you, by the way," Shaunna said.

"Have you?"

"Yeah. But let's finish our drinks first. You'll probably drop your cup otherwise."

Andy made puppy-dog eyes at her. She just smiled.

"Wait and see!"

He huffed impatiently.

"Don't get in a sulk," she chastised.

"I don't sulk!"

"What was all that drinking about the other night if not sulking?"

"I was wallowing in—what's it called? Unrequited love?"

Shaunna tilted her head and examined him but didn't comment. When they'd finished their hot chocolate, she set both cups on the floor and knelt next to him, so they were facing each other, and took his hand. He laced his fingers through hers.

"It's not unrequited," she said, lifting his chin so he had to meet her gaze. She leaned forward and kissed him gently on the lips. "I love you," she whispered.

His heart skipped a beat. "Could you say that again?"

She held his gaze. "I love you. Happy now?"

He laughed and kissed her back. "Yeah. I couldn't be any happier."

"I wouldn't bank on it."

Andy gave her an enquiring look, but her expression told him nothing. "This other present, then?" he prompted.

She smiled. "Well, it *is* small and doesn't cost a lot…"

He raised an eyebrow.

"At the moment."

"OK?" He frowned, intrigued.

She freed her fingers from his and placed his palm against her belly, watching him as the meaning of her actions sank in.

"You're…"

She nodded.

"Since when?"

"I did the tests four days ago. That was the other reason I was so angry with you for standing me up at the electronics store. I didn't know what I was going to do, and I needed to talk to you about it."

Pain flickered across his face, and she squeezed his other hand.

"I wouldn't have got rid of it. I just wasn't sure how I was going to tell Kris without him doing something crazy. I'm still worried about telling Adele and Dan."

"Fair enough." Andy could understand that. He'd been on his way home from a London business trip when he'd heard Adele had miscarried, and it had hit Dan really hard. Eleven months down the line, Dan and Adele were still trying for another baby, and with them both turning forty in the coming year, there was a sense that time was running out. Whilst Andy hoped with all his heart that it worked out for them soon, he'd never been one to feel guilty for his own good fortune. He closed his eyes and smiled, his palm still resting on Shaunna's belly. "I think they'll be pleased for us."

"I hope so." She chewed her lip thoughtfully. She wasn't looking forward to breaking the news to everyone else. "So anyway, I have a feeling I'm about three months along."

"How does...ah." His shoulders sagged as it dawned on him that maybe it wasn't his after all.

"Oh, it's definitely yours," she confirmed, "but the dates are based on the first day of your last period, and I can't remember having one since—" She didn't want to say what she'd been about to say. "Since the beginning of October."

"It happened the first time?"

Shaunna shrugged and returned to her previous position, cuddled up beside him. Still his hand remained on her belly. "Yeah, well, that's what you get for leaving contraception to the man," she teased.

"I told you. I wanted you to have my baby."

"Don't start that again, or we'll end up having another argument."

"Sorry." Andy kissed her head. "You were right, though. I should've talked to you about it rather than hoping it might happen by accident."

"Yes, you should," Shaunna agreed. "Because then you'd have found out I was hoping the same."

"Funny," he remarked.

"What?"

"Sexist, I think you called me?"

"Misogynist, actually. I changed my mind."

"I convinced you otherwise?"

"Nope. Woman's prerogative."

He nodded, smirking mischievously. "In that case," he said, "I think it's time for a bit of man's prerogative." He slowly eased forward, keeping his arms around her as he gently lowered her to the floor and came down on top of her, smoothing her hair with his fingers and delivering tender, soft-lipped kisses.

"I was right about the other bit as well," she said.

"What's that?"

"You really are hopelessly romantic." She ran her palms down his back, trying to pull him closer.

"And *you* are insatiable, but we have a date. Just you, me and a rug in front of a roaring fire."

"So we do. All we're missing is the—"

She didn't get any further than that, as he'd thought ahead and left the marshmallows within easy reach. He fed one to her, and she pushed her mouth against his, the heat of their kiss instantly melting the sweet and sticking their lips together. They continued to kiss and giggle until all of the sugary residue was gone, leaving in its place an intense quietness but for the crackle and flicker of the log fire. Andy rolled onto his side and wrapped his arms around her, carefully removing the clip from her hair and kissing her at the same time.

"Merry Christmas, RHB."

"Merry Christmas, sexy."

THE END

About the Author

Debbie McGowan is an author and publisher based in a semi-rural corner of Lancashire, England. She writes character-driven, realist fiction, celebrating life, love and relationships. A working-class girl, she 'ran away' to London at seventeen, was homeless, unemployed and then homeless again, interspersed with animal rights activism (all legal, honest ;)) and volunteer work as a mental health advocate. At twenty-five, she went back to college to study social science—tough with two toddlers, but they had a 'stay at home' dad, so it worked itself out. These days, the toddlers are young women (much to their chagrin) and Debbie teaches undergraduate students, writes novels and runs an independent publishing company, occasionally grabbing an hour's sleep where she can.

Social Media Links

Website: debbiemcgowan.co.uk and hidingbehindthecouch.com
Newsletter Signup: eepurl.com/b8emHL
Blog: deb248211.blogspot.com
Facebook: facebook.com/DebbieMcGowanAuthor and facebook.com/beatentrackpublishing
Twitter: @writerdebmcg
YouTube: youtube.com/deb248211
Instagram: instagram/writerdebmcg
Tumblr: writerdebmcg.tumblr.com
LinkedIn: uk.linkedin.com/in/writerdebmcg
Goodreads: goodreads.com/DebbieMcGowan
Books2Read: books2read.com/DebbieMcGowan

By the Author

I'm not a single-genre author, for which I make no apology. Nor do I write stories of a specific length; I believe a story should be as long as it needs to be.

Thus, to assist you in navigating my catalogue, I've also included the closest-fitting genres and types of publication.

Hiding Behind The Couch Series
(Contemporary/Literary Fiction)
The ongoing story of 'The Circle'...
Nine friends from high school;
Nine friends for life.

The Story So Far...
(in chronological order)

- *Beginnings* (Novella)
- *Ruminations* (Novel)
- *Class-A* (Short Story – also in *Take a Chance* anthology)
- *Hiding Behind The Couch* (Season One)
- *No Time Like The Present* (Season Two)
- *The Harder They Fall* (Season Three)
- *Crying in the Rain* (Novel)
- *First Christmas* (Novella)
- *In The Stars Part I: Capricorn–Gemini* (Season Four)
- *Breaking Waves* (Novella)
- *Chain of Secrets* (Novella – also in Love Unlocked anthology)
- *In The Stars Part II: Cancer–Sagittarius* (Season Five)
- *A Midnight Clear* (Novella – also in *Boughs of Evergreen* anthology)
- **Red Hot Christmas** (Novella)

- *Two By Two* (Season Six)
- *Hiding Out* (Novella – CHO Crossover)
- *Those Jeffries Boys* (Novel)
- *The WAG and The Scoundrel* (Gray Fisher #1)
- *Perfect Tenor* (Novella)
- *The Lost Mitten* (see 'Children's Stories')
- *Reunions* (Season Seven)
- *Tabula Rasa* (Gray Fisher #2)
- *Breakfast at Cordelia's Aquarium* (Short Story)
- *Reverberations* (Novel)
- *To Be Sure* (Novella – also in *Never Too Late* anthology)
- *What A Scorcher!* (Flash Fiction)
- *Goth of Christmas Past* (Front of House #1)
- ***The Advent of Reason*** (**Novella**)
- *Not My Christmas* (Novella)
- *Highlights* ~ co-written with A.M. Leibowitz (Short Story – Notes from Boston meets Hiding Behind The Couch)
- *Distractions* (Gray Fisher #3)

Checking Him Out Series
(M/M and LGBTQ Romance)

- *Checking Him Out* (Book One)
- *Checking Him Out For the Holidays* (Novella)
- *Hiding Out* (Novella – Noah and Matty – HBTC Crossover)
- *Taking Him On* (Book Two – Noah and Matty)
- *Checking In* (Book Three)
- *The Making of Us* (Book Four – Jesse and Leigh)

Seeds of Tyrone Series
(M/M Romance)

~ co-written with Raine O'Tierney

- *Leaving Flowers* (Book One)
- *Where the Grass is Greener* (Book Two)
- *Christmas Craic and Mistletoe* (Book Three)

Stand-Alone Stories

- *Champagne* (LGBTQ Historical Novel)
- 'Time to Go' (Contemporary Short in *Story Salon Big Book of Stories*)
- *And The Walls Came Tumbling Down* (Sci-fi Novel)
- *No Dice* (Sci-fi Novel)
- *Double Six* (Sci-fi Novel)
- *Sugar and Sawdust* (M/M Romance Short Story)
- *Cherry Pop Valentine* (M/M Romance Short Story)
- *Coming Up* ~ co-written with Al Stewart (LGBTQ Short Story)
- *Of the Bauble* (LGBTQ Fantasy Romance Novella)
- *So Long, Little Black Diamonds* (True Short Story)
- *The Pastor's Last Drop* (Ongoing Historical Novel – Wattpad)
- *When Skies Have Fallen* (LGBTQ Historical Romance Novel)
- *A Snowy Ball* (When Skies Have Fallen Novelette)
- *The Great Village Bun Fight* (LGBTQ Comedy Novella – also in *Seasons of Love* anthology)
- 'Oh No She Didn't!' (LGBTQ Short Story in *Upstaged!: an anthology of women who love women in the performing arts*)
- *The Great Pretendo* (Flash Fiction)
- 'Nina, Pretty Ballerina' (Short Story in *Play On…: a collection of short stories, poetry and prose, inspired by the songs of ABBA*)
- *Meredith's Dagger* (Contemporary/Historical Feminist/LGBTQ Novel)

Audiobooks

- *And The Walls Came Tumbling Down* – Narrated by Hannibal Mills
- *Checking Him Out* – Narrated by Tim Larkfield
- *Of The Bauble* – Narrated by Jack Hardman
- *The Great Village Bun Fight* – Narrated by Jack Hardman
- *When Skies Have Fallen* – Narrated by Tim Holbourne

Children's Stories (written as J.S. Morley)

- *The Lost Mitten* ~ illustrated by Sofia Oxelstrand
- *Chompy the Velociraptor* ~ illustrated by Kate Andrew
- *Zoom the Pterodactyl*

www.debbiemcgowan.co.uk

Beaten Track Publishing

For more titles from Beaten Track Publishing,
please visit our website:

https://www.beatentrackpublishing.com

Thanks for reading!